FATALLY FLAWED

ANATOMY OF A PRESIDENT

ROBERT LISLE

First hardback edition December 2022
First paperback edition December 2022
First eBook edition January 2023

First published in the United States in 2022
by IngramSpark Publishing.
Hardcover: 979-8-9865614-0-0
Paperback: 979-8-9865614-1-7
eBook: 979-8-9865614-2-4

Edited by C Y Gopinath
Cover and book design by C Y Gopinath

Typeset in Adobe Caslon 11.5 / 17 pt

www.fatallyflawed.org

To Nancy

What Critics Are Saying

Fatally Flawed is by turns both global and intimate in its scale, resulting in a thoughtfully crafted and eminently enjoyable first novel. Robert Lisle shares an engrossing character study in the dynamics of personal, professional, and political power – and the potential for that power to be corrupted – in a literary thriller that delivers a knockout of an ending.

Jonathan Haupt
Executive Director
Pat Conroy Literary Center

Creative, captivating and instructive in a way readers may find familiar. Fatally Flawed packs a wallop while Lisle keeps you on the edge of your seat. This one will stay with you long after you close the book because of what you glean between the lines.

Marilyn Arseneau,
Educator, Book Club maven

Readers hungry for a rich stew of political intrigue seasoned by a beautiful Lebanese seductress and brought to a boil by a master storyteller will savor Fatally Flawed to its thrilling conclusion.

John Warley
Author of *The Home Guard*

Fatally Flawed is an enjoyable, easy-to-read page-turner that touches on a vast array of subjects, from the narcissism of a young football star to the tragedy of dementia, from the shenanigans of national politics to the rise of international terrorism (Lisle traces anti-Americanism back to Lebanon in an interesting way). The plot twists will keep you engaged and guessing, and the ending will leave you wondering: 'So – is this how it might have happened?'

Deno P. Trakas
Author of *Messenger from Mystery*
Professor Emeritus, Department of English and
Director of Creative Writing, Wofford College

Contents

911

"9-1-1, what is your emergency?"

The female dispatcher's voice was cool and controlled. The old man's was just the opposite, hoarse and urgent. Words tumbled out of his mouth in a torrent.

"Please slow down, sir. May I have your name?"

"My name is not important!" he said, agitated. "The country is in danger!"

The middle-aged dispatcher pushed her hair away from her face and adjusted her hands-free headset. She was used to calls like this, and years of practice had taught her that in such situations nothing worked quite as well as a steady tone and infinite patience.

"We still need your name, sir," she said. "Could you please spell it out for me?"

"Look," the old man bristled, "I'm not the criminal mastermind here. But there's something very strange going down next door — and I'm sure it spells trouble for America!"

"I need you to calm down, sir, so that I can get all the details," she said, still calm and professional. "Can you tell me where exactly this 'next door' is, sir? Where precisely are you?"

"Listen, miss, it's these Arab fellows — well, I'm guessing they're Arabs but they could be from any of those dangerous countries."

"Sir, would you mind starting with your location?"

"Yes, sure thing. I'm in the fourth brownstone on the block. There's a row of brownstones, see, they've been here a long time — so I'm in the fourth one, and they're right next door —"

"Sir, sir, sir," the operator said patiently. "Please slow down just a little. Which city are you in at the moment?"

"Look, miss, I'm not sure how much time we have left. Yesterday one of them chased me with a knife. Me and my little poodle spent all last night under my staircase hiding from them."

A small crowd had gathered around the dispatcher. Everyone sensed this might be more than a crank call. It was vital to keep the old man talking so that they could activate a trace.

"Where did you say your house was, sir?"

"That's not the point, young lady! You're not hearing me. When I saw these same guys at the café, they kept mentioning some house that is white — and they really had an accent, believe me."

The circular wall-clock hung like a moon looking over the tightly cubicled office space in Baltimore, Maryland, filled with 911 emergency dispatchers. The night shift would be over in just 40 minutes but the last eight hours had been especially busy. A Saturday night at Christmas time, no surprise there, she thought: the typical festival of human misadventures, from a row house fire in Hamden and a dust-up at the Horse You Came In On Saloon to a front-seat baby boy delivery on the way to Mercy Hospital.

"Do you think they were talking about the White House, sir?"

"That's it!" cried the voice at the other end. "That's exactly it! How could I have missed it?"

"Sir, this sounds very serious — do you mind if we could start over, more slowly this time."

"Yes, yes, whatever you say. Just do it fast, we don't have any time to lose. They're already loading things into the funny-looking bus they repainted yesterday."

"Right — now then, let's start again with your name, shall we?"

There was a long silence at the other end.

"Sir? Are you still there?"

"Oy vey!" the man said, agitated again. "You know, I

think these nasty guys are heading toward the White House with bombs — and all you want to know is my name? You know what? Meshuggeneh! I'm done with this."

Then, with a click, he hung up.

Clutch & Co

Click!

Ernest Thomas Haynes, ET to his friends, cranked his faithful Rolleiflex to the next frame, having caught the unforgettable face in his viewfinder.

"Got it."

The Falls Church High Jaguar's cheerleaders, dressed in game day green and white, ogled the stunning captain of their high school football team as he posed for the camera. They had begun calling this near perfect Adonis 'Clutch' as a 14-year-old freshman — and the nickname had stuck. Clearly, when the genes for the most desirable physical attributes were being distributed, Sir Clutch had gotten almost all of them. From the waves in his fiery-blond hair to the classic Roman nose and chiseled cheeks, his face bordered on perfection, to say nothing of his imposing height and powerful physique. Anyone paying attention would say Lance had indeed hit the genetic jackpot. Girls were known to gasp at the sight of him and then turn away with embarrassment for fear his polar blue eyes would catch them staring.

They could not have known that Clutch had forgotten to take his medication that morning, which often left him a bit drowsy. It was frightening for him to remember that as far back as early childhood his allergies could trigger a potentially life-threatening asthma attack. Needless to say, Clutch kept this medical vulnerability a closely guarded secret though he had realized that on occasion he could leverage it for personal benefit. Such as doing only five wind sprints instead of ten after practice. Indeed, fall ragweed and spring pine pollen could sometimes be put to good use.

ET looked at him. "You like it ?"

"It's a beauty," said Clutch, looking at the photo. "Love that angle. May I keep it?"

ET gave him the 8" x 10" black-and-white print. "Here you go. Enjoy!"

"You're becoming a bit of a photographic legend around here, you know."

ET smiled modestly. "Think you might be making a career out of it?

Indeed, photography and ET had bonded early. The

romance had started at the age of nine when his parents had gifted him his first camera, a Kodak Brownie, as he left for "sleep away camp". The gadget had quickly become his pride and joy, and he had relished clicking beautiful landscapes, fun-filled camp activities and the many smiling faces of the new friends he had made that summer.

It was inevitable that when he entered ninth grade, ET would become his high school's class photographer. Working on the school newspaper and the class yearbook, the young shutterbug tirelessly captured all aspects of student life. He took all the formal yearbook senior portraits as well as countless action photographs of school sporting events and extracurricular activities. It gave him immeasurable pleasure and also insights into the repertoire of human behavior. He grew more comfortable focusing on his subjects through the viewfinder of his camera. He was a natural.

There was at least one who was more eager than others to seek out photographic self -promotion.

"I feel so myself before your camera." This from Sir Clutch himself.

Indeed, the captain and starting quarterback of the winningest football team in school history with his jersey number being the first ever to be retired had come to enjoy the photographic attention. The debate team had also excelled under his leadership, with a striking ET photograph of him pointing a finger at his audience, almost suggesting that each one there should just go ahead and agree with his point of view no matter how preposterous it might be.

No real surprise, then, that Clutch's talents and charisma propelled him right up to the position of president of his senior class, and also the student council. Nor was it a surprise that all the most attractive girls clamored to be photographed near him and secretly dreamed of being his homecoming queen.

Except, ET noted, for one lass named Katherine, "Kat" for short. ET had become intrigued by her preference for privacy and her apparent indifference to being photographed, which had only made her that much more interesting to him.

It was the final school bell for the week. This Friday afternoon at Falls Church High was meant for hanging out with buddies before the football game began that evening. Kat reached up to open her locker to put her books away and ET spotted her, his camera at the ready.

She turned and looked at him.

"May I?" ET asked politely.

Kat's lips tightened. Was she welcoming him or annoyed? He couldn't tell.

Click.

"Thank you! Front page stuff!" ET said with a contagious grin.

And that started it. Their conversation came out of nowhere and flowed as naturally as a winding brook through the rest of the afternoon.

"...I can't stand the Beatles..."

"...Then I bet you like Simon and Garfunkel.."

"...Oh no I don't..."

"...I can see you're hard to figure out. A mystery girl!"

"...I can dance to the Supremes..."

"...Now on that we both agree..."

High five.

"...Tell me you don't like Andy Warhol..."

"...Who?"

Their voices, now animated, now soft, were interspersed with flirtatious laughter.

"...How about Sam Cookes' *You Send Me?*..."

"...I do?..."

"...Honest you do!..."

Chuckles.

"...Do you think that *Love Story* flick is based on a true story?..."

"...Why would I care about that, Mystery Girl?..."

"...You mean you don't like Ali McGraw..."

"Not saying that," ET's voice stumbled. "I mean that whole thing about love at first sight..."

Kat pounced right on it. "Well, what about love at first sight?"

Down the hall, Clutch pulled his ball cap from his locker, looking with growing interest at the couple waving reluctant goodbyes to each other. He waited for Kat to go out the door before moving in on ET.

"Looks like you have a crush going on, my man."

ET smiled. "She seems very nice."

It's A Deal!

ET had been delighted by the call from Clutch earlier that week.

"You'll love it! You and your camera will go crazy here. The Billy Goat Trail is loaded with scenic views."

They left early Sunday morning. Clutch drove north on Interstate 495 into Maryland and exited onto Route 190 heading west. Traffic was light and they made good time.

ET, loading a new roll of film into his camera, turned toward Clutch. "Nice game Friday, by the way. Six and O. Go Jags —I got some good pics."

Achoo! Achoo! Clutch groped for the tissues, eyes suddenly watering.

"You okay?" ET asked.

"I'll be fine, thanks," said Clutch with a slight wheeze.

"They didn't have much of a defense."

"You're not sounding great, buddy," said ET.

"Damn ragweed — I should have taken my medicines before we left."

"Anyway, I think you picked them apart."

Clutch closed the driver's side window, eyes still watering but pleased with the compliment as he pulled into a parking space. He reached into his backpack's side pocket and pulled out a plastic vial of pills.

"Buzzingo! This is it — the Great Falls of the Potomac, one of the D.C. area's most spectacular natural landmarks!"

Indeed, the trail was as challenging as predicted but manageable, and the two young men ventured forth enjoying the breathtaking scenery. The lookout was positioned 100 feet above the powerful rapids of the Potomac River with a dramatic stretch of steep tiered cascades to the south. As they stood in silence admiring the view, Clutch's breathing eased and the two hikers settled into comfortable conversation. An hour passed quickly.

"It may be a stretch but I'm hoping the Naval Academy will come through," said ET. "My congressman thinks I've got a good shot."

"Maybe they need a good photographer."

"My family would have been proud."

"Would have been?" Clutch raised an eyebrow.

ET reached behind and pulled out a wallet from his jeans pocket and extracted a laminated photograph to show Clutch — the smiling faces of his parents and only sister, all standing together, one happy family, at the entrance to Disneyland.

"They died one month after this was taken."

"What happened?" urged Clutch.

"They were on a missionary trip to West Africa. We'd always been good churchgoers and dad felt the 'call' to spread the lord's word in a small village north of Monrovia, the capital of a country called Liberia."

Clutch nodded, listening.

"Some kind of crazy virus spread by a mosquito," ET continued. "The minister and congregation who sponsored the trip have never forgiven themselves. I still wonder whether stateside emergency measures might have saved their lives. Eighteen people died."

"And you — survived?"

ET shook his head, "I didn't go. I was struggling with reading —something called dyslexia. My folks thought I best stay home and work with a tutor."

He took another sip of his Coke and continued with his story. "Growing up, life was good. Dad had a steady job as a mechanic — or 'auto technician', as he liked to call it. He had a bunch of genuine buddies who would do anything for him. But dad was proud of being self-sufficient. And boy was he a snuggler. The whole family was always getting these gentle, endless, loving hugs."

Clutch had learned that the best way to get someone

talking was to stay quiet. People love to fill silences with their own words.

"We called Mom the 'Enforcer'. She ruled with an iron hand but not without a light touch. Her role was clear — internal household operations. Mom expected a lot from us. She had no time and zero tolerance for bad behavior but she sure gave me some healthy aspirations." ET knew that his family had a lot to do with the young man he had become, someone who could handle whatever knuckleballs life threw his way.

"She did a good job, buddy."

ET took a final swig of his Coke. Enough family disclosure, he thought.

A soft breeze massaged the colorful autumn trees behind the two young men.

"Me, I got all my eggs in one basket," said Clutch. "West Point needs a quarterback and the football coach there says he's got some pull. And my congresswoman — I think she's got the hots for me."

"Ha," laughed ET. "Sounds like a done deal."

"She's a looker too! I went to her office at the Capitol. Special pass and all."

"Let me guess. She couldn't take her eyes off you?"

Clutch smiled smugly. "And what about you?"

"What do you mean?"

"You got a girlfriend?"

"Well, I'm trying —" ET trailed off, not sure that he

wanted to talk about this.

"You mean Katherine?" pressed Clutch.

ET flushed.. "There sure is something special about her. Her looks, the way she talks to me, her sense of humor —"

"Sounds serious, dude."

"She's just so busy all the time. And hell, I really don't have any idea how she feels about me."

"Shazam!" said Clutch, with a flourish. "Guess what? Kat and I go way back. Just say the word and I could set up some, well, opportunities for you two to 'accidentally' bump into each other."

"Could you really?"

"Sure I could," said Clutch. He held out his index finger. "But there's a condition."

ET smiled. "There always is."

"You become my official photographer till the end of school. I want every moment recorded, everything I do, every event, every expression, every detail."

ET thought for a moment. That sounded a little weird — but what the heck. He reached out to shake hands.

"You got a deal, Captain Clutch!"

Love Shot

"Ansel Adams! Step aside!"

The art teacher overseeing the production of the class year-book looked down at the scattering of photographs on the large round table.

"You're quite the master, young man," he said. "The quality, the sensitivity, the way you spot beauty in your subjects!"

"Been at it a while, sir," said ET, who had never been a fan of undue attention.

"The students love your exhibition in the cafeteria."

ET grinned modestly. "Distracts them from the rubber chicken, I bet!"

"I took my class for a closer look at your work yesterday after lunch," the teacher said. "Boy, were they overwhelmed."

ET smiled. "Glad to hear that, sir."

"Just so happens that an old college classmate of mine is

now the curator of photographs at the National Geographic Museum and Gallery."

ET was suddenly very interested. Some of the best photographers in the world worked there.

"How do you like the idea of displaying some of your work there and maybe giving a talk on the history of photography?"

ET felt his heart pounding, his face flushed.

"I'll take that as a yes," said the teacher, eyes twinkling.

The huge automatic doors opened with mechanical authority and ET entered the massive lobby of the National Geographic Society's headquarters, noting immediately the large cluster of people milling about.

"ET Haynes, welcome!" said the smartly dressed young curator with the bright red horn-rimmed glasses.

Clearing his throat, ET took a deep breath and grinned, awash with delight at the large crowd that included so many of his classmates.

"I love talking about photography — as you can probably tell," he began without preamble. "It's been my consuming passion for as long as I can remember. However, I do realize that some of you might find what I have to say no more interesting than a wilting houseplant." Laughter rippled through the gathering.

ET began by posing a question, hoping that at least a few of those present would still be with him when he reached the end of his presentation.

"Did you know that photography was introduced to the world the very same year that congress outlawed dueling as a way of settling an argument on these very streets of Washington, DC?"

Several sets of eyes immediately glazed over.

With a smile towards those still paying attention, ET answered his own question. "The year was 1839 — the official birth year of photography."

The next hour went by quickly as he and his entourage moved through the timeline display of photographs and photographic artifacts from the museum's collection. ET's voice rose enthusiastically as he pointed to a small black box in one of the showcases. "In 1888, the first Kodak camera was born right here in America. It democratized photography! An easy-to-use box camera was now available for every man, woman and child!"

To the right, in a pastel sundress stood Kat, attentive and looking beautiful. ET caught her eye and she winked back.

"Thank you all for your attention. Are there any questions?"

Kat's hand went up. "Where do you get your inspiration?"

ET looked at her and paused, barely concealing the huge grin that wanted to cover his face.

"From people like you."

The crowd tittered, enjoying his answer. ET dramatically put his hand to his heart, still staring at Kat, and drew another friendly wave of laughter.

ET left the museum elated that he had at least given a few students a better sense of their own cameras' ancestry. What excited him more, however, was the fact that some of the students actually 'got' how potent their camera could be as a tool for self-expression and self-discovery. And Kat was one of them.

"You embarrassed me today, you know," Kat said, looking straight at ET later that afternoon.

"Do you have a problem with the truth, miss?" ET replied, patting his chest again.

Kat cocked her head, "Are you flirting with me?"

"Any chance I get."

Kat brushed a lock of gleaming auburn hair away from her cheek. The warm appeal of her face lay in its subtle imperfections and ET loved them. The slightly turned up nose, the cheeks sprinkled with some mild freckling and the narrow gap between her two front teeth somehow became her. Growing up, this unusual dental configuration had actually afforded her the unique ability of whistling louder than any of the boys and won her membership among their ranks.

"Did Clutch put you up to coming today?"

"What do you mean?"

"Has he been pushing you in my direction?"

"Not without my agreement. But Lord knows that man can be a bully."

ET looked curious.

"You do know he's my brother, right?"

ET's jaw dropped.

"I had no idea. What a sly fox. He told me he could arrange meetings so we could be together — but only in exchange for my taking photos of him for the rest of our time in school."

"That's my brother, always quietly working an angle. He

mostly hides it well but good old Lance has quite the devious streak. He's the great manipulator in the family."

"Lance?"

"Yeppers. Lance Allworthy, my brother. That's him, Sir Lancelot himself — savior of damsels!"

"So what's with the nickname Clutch?"

"Maybe it came from a wannabe girlfriend or some teammate who admired his athletic prowess in the clutch," Kat continued. "Most folks have no idea he can be such a meany."

ET shook his head.

"My poor sister, Cleo. He was so nasty to her growing up that she ended up going to a different high school just to be away from him. He used to call her Ugly Hester and Spinster Girl and was always playing hurtful pranks on her like hiding her shoes or stealing her homework."

"Which you escaped?"

"Tough skin and a good counter punch."

Indeed, Kat had somehow skipped her brother's mean genes and had quite miraculously emerged as a caring and forgiving soul. She was genuine and fun-loving, with a natural gift for making friends. Her eager mind found favor with those around her and while she had all the makings of sass and pretense, she had not the slightest inclination to use them.

ET reached out and touched her arm. "So you came today without coercion?"

Kat smiled enigmatically.

"Maybe," she said.

Parallel Lives

"And so, my fellow classmates, here we are."

The light wind tugged at the fringes of Lance's golden hair as he stood behind the podium. The tassels blew atop his mortarboard cap as he looked out at the audience of faculty, friends and fellow seniors. "On this much-awaited day, let the spotlight shine on each and every one of us as our high school days come to a close and we move on to the next chapters of our lives."

ET and Kat had elected to sit together in the front row with some reluctance. Of course Lance had asked him to bring his camera to the graduation ceremony. ET turned toward Kat, shrugged and winked; Kat shrugged back.

The program moved forward with the principal of the school now announcing standout individuals whom the class had voted as somehow special.

"Most Likely to Succeed goes to — soon-to-be Cadet — Lance Allworthy." Applause.

"Soon-to-be-Plebe — Ernest Thomas Haynes, a classmate with Outstanding Talent outside the classroom." ET turned around to the audience and raised his camera in the air. Raucous applause.

"Last but not least, by unanimous consent this year's Most Popular Senior award goes to Katherine Allworthy." A standing ovation.

ET slipped his arm around her back and pulled her towards him, whispering, "A fine choice indeed!"

The Falls Church Jaguar fight song closed the ceremony. The students quickly removed their caps and gowns under the hot sun of a mid-June Virginia day and began to mingle amidst a communal chorus of congratulations. It was a moment mixed with tears and hugs along with emotional signings of the high school yearbook. Clutch was surrounded by fellow students wanting his autograph underneath his picture. Many girls secretly hoped he might write something uniquely personal in their yearbooks. Lance loved the attention. "Maybe y'all should make a line."

ET stepped up and pushed his yearbook at Lance for an autograph and maybe some words of appreciation.

"So your congresswoman didn't let you down, Lance! Congratulations!" ET reached out to shake his hand. He took silent pleasure in the fact that he was among the 8%

of applicants that had been admitted to the Naval Academy while 12% of applicants had gotten into West Point.

"Congratulations to you too!" said Lance. "Looks like Army gets a quarterback and Navy gets a photographer."

The message from Lance in ET's yearbook was brief.

Hey Plebe,
Perhaps our paths will cross again.
Maybe the Army-Navy game.

Clutch

Kat turned to face ET and handed him her yearbook and a pen. He found the page with her portrait on it. He thought for only a moment before writing —

The Naval Academy is just a hop and a
skip over the Severn River from College
Park. This isn't goodbye, my love.

Yours, ET

ET handed the open yearbook back to Kat who read the words he'd just written. A tear slid down her cheek.

"Your turn."

Kat found his portrait and wrote underneath it.

To my midshipman, sweethearts we are
with no expiration date! I'll release you to
the Naval Academy but only temporarily.

XOXO, Kat

The two embraced and kissed before noticing Cleo approaching with another young woman. "Welcome to our celebration!" said Kat. "I'd like you to meet ET, my —"

"Sweetheart." Cleo finished the sentence for her sister with a smile.

"Have you seen big brother Lance?"

Katherine pointed toward him. "He's busy giving people the opportunity to congratulate him!"

"Hey, am I surprised! Valedictorian and football captain! Too bad the guy's a jerk," Cleo bristled.

Heavy clouds had crept up and blackened the sky. Suddenly a clap of thunder and rain came pouring down, causing a stampede for cover as people scrambled to shelter within the school building. Lance ran to the classroom where the debate team usually met, the seats being more comfortable there. The downpour lasted an hour.

Something familiar caught his eye. He squinted for better focus and recognized his sister Cleo, in an alcove to the rear of the room behind a mobile blackboard. She was locked in an embrace with a young girl he did not recognize.

"Cleo," he called out.

The startled couple disentangled as Lance approached. "My, my, sis. I see you're having fun. Have I met your friend? Or would you rather add her name to the secrets you keep from the family?"

Lance Allworthy obsessively dedicated the six short remaining weeks of summer to fine-tuning his body at the local health club, while ET spent the same time hopelessly in love with Kat. It was a time of kisses, laughter, music and holding hands. The two agreed that James Taylor probably said it best: *How Sweet It Is To Be Loved By You*.

Or was it good old Sam Cooke's *You Send Me* the young lovers chimed?

"Honest I do!"

"You do?"

The two were together all the time except during ET's hours at the uptown camera shop developing prints and selling cameras while Kat worked at the local art supply store. Kat wouldn't let ET forget the level of physical fitness required of a freshman at the Naval Academy. After 40 push-ups, she embraced his upper arm, pulling him close. "Nice muscle there, fella."

Kat rode beside him on her bike when he ran, checking her stopwatch every 30 seconds. The 6-minute mile cadet requirement was ET's biggest challenge. The swimming requirement was less Draconian, involving training twice a week at the beach. The two lovers combined bobbing in the surf with an all-out sprint to the end of the jetty. Thus did summer end.

And then, one day, the shuttle came to take ET away.

He had only seconds to say goodbye to Kat before boarding. She buried herself in his arms, contemplating no verbal or physical contact for seven weeks. Tears rolled down her cheeks; ET controlled his. Midshipmen don't cry.

Leaving the civilian world for four years was what ET had signed up for and he was prepared to embrace it to the fullest, no matter what. From tight bed corners and having to jog everywhere he went on campus to barking "Beat Army" before the evening meal. I'm all in, ET said to himself on his way to his first Seamanship and Navigation class, to be followed by water polo practice.

Prayers before lunch. Food's pretty good!

Weights, pull-ups and crunches and then run a mile.

More classes, eating and evening studies.

And it all starts over again at 5.30 the next morning.

"Blue and Gold, anchors aweigh!"

West Point welcomed the trim, well-conditioned Lance. The towering Gothic Old Cadet Chapel, built in 1916, set the tone for the rest of the greystone buildings around the campus. George Washington had seen the location as a perfect defense position against the British, with its southeast view overlooking the Hudson River.

Lance's new home for the next 47 months would require him to make a variety of adjustments. He had been unprepared for the humiliation of someone buzzing off all his golden hair in less than 60 seconds. Gone also was the blind adoration he'd received wherever he went in high school. I'm not used to this, he thought as he got off the bus to the stentorian blast from a drill sergeant he would grow to hate.

Cleaning toilets, asking permission to eat, setting the table for upperclassmen was bad enough. The worst thing was taking orders from someone else.

Nevertheless Lance Allworthy's outward persona radiated a charisma born of his undisputed natural instinct to lead a football team to victory. It certainly helped that he could do 20 one-handed push-ups, putting the 900 cadets in his entering class in an almost immediate state of awe, admiration and envy.

Lance soon determined that the military and academic curricula could be managed like everything else in his life thus far, though some new challenges were imposed by the rigid code of honor that governed all activities at West Point. Cadet Allworthy met these with agile if sometimes morally elastic behavior, skillfully escaping any significant military tarnish. When so much of the spotlight had already come to him without any great personal effort, he found himself becoming less dedicated, at least in areas he perceived as being irrelevant or even ridiculous. Such as certain marching drills. Or disassembling a .22 caliber bolt action rifle in the dark. Or the art of a proper salute. Nevertheless he pursued the obligatory activities with feigned enthusiasm, taking care not to risk sabotaging his own personal ambitions.

Fellow cadets who might have known of his sometimes slightly loose behavior chose to look the other way. No one dared to openly criticize Lance's flexible ethics. After all, his absolute importance to the Army football team was undisputed and by now common knowledge. An unbroken record of victories and a sound thrashing of Navy's Cinderella season was on the mind of most every cadet and faculty officer right on up to the members of West Point's board of directors.

Victory this season rested on Lance's shoulders. And anyone who was paying attention knew it.

Augusta

The day of the game broke late-autumn fresh over Michie Stadium, the home of Army's football team. The brilliant foliage of upstate New York had commenced its reluctant surrender to the early chill of approaching winter. As families everywhere gathered around their Thanksgiving turkeys, West Point and its surroundings hummed with football mania over the upcoming afternoon game in the famous stadium alongside the Hudson River. While traditionally played in Philadelphia, this year's Army-Navy American classic would be waged on the home field of the Army's Black Knights.

The media was all over it, calling it the culmination of the most magical season in college football history. Both Army and Navy had undefeated, superbly coached teams and speculation raged as to which one of these two power-houses was going to capture the win. Sportscasters had all the facts and figures they needed to spout their individual predictions and analyses. Perhaps not surprisingly, Las Vegas had put its money on Army, presumably based on the superlative talents of its quarterback Lance Allworthy.

The young gridiron hero was quick-timing it from Bancroft Hall, the largest dormitory in the world, towards the stadium where he would perform that afternoon. He had taken his medication two hours earlier and was feeling no adverse side-effects.

His gray hoodie read *Sink Navy* across the front. Its drawstring was tight around his red cheeks. The big game with Navy didn't start until 1, with the fly-past of six F-18 fighter jets, but some hardcore patrons had already found their parking spots and were prepping for a pre-game tailgate party. Lance wove through the maze of vehicles; somewhere at hand he smelt a charcoal grill firing up.

"Ribs won't be ready till noon," someone called out.

Not breaking his stride, Lance entered the stadium through Gate 5, which took him to the Army side of the field. Showing the attendant his laminated student ID, he stopped to pull his Canon SureShot point-and-shoot camera from his sweatshirt pocket and took several outside shots of the empty stadium, one of the oldest and finest in the country. In three hours, it would be brimming with close to 40,000 people, and more than half the fans would be cheering for him to the tune of On, Brave Old Army Team.

He turned and double-timed back to the exit through the same gate where most of the top brass Army officials and well-heeled alumni would sit, saluting the attendant as he passed. That was when he heard the muffled scream of a woman. "Please. . . please, stop!"

Lance looked in the direction of the sound, instinctively raising his camera. From somewhere behind a metal scaffolding came sounds of a struggle. Partly hidden was a large man in a full dress Army uniform. A woman was pushing him away. One of his hands was tight in her hair, pulling her head back as he tried to kiss her, while the other groped her breast.

"Stop — you monster –"

Click. Click. Lance began striding towards the couple. Hearing the camera's shutter, the startled man let go of the woman's hair, straightening up to face the oncoming Lance.

A voice called out from behind him. "Hey you, what are you, some kind of voyeur?" Lance turned to see another army man, a major by the looks of him.

"Neither sir, just a photo for the record," he said lightly. "Some pre-game views."

Two women drew up behind the major, clearly mother and daughter. "What's going on, Major Sedgwick?" the older woman asked.

The major was in Lance's face now, red with outrage. "Certain things are private, you know."

The flustered couple had taken advantage of the confrontation between Lance and the major to collect themselves and straighten out their clothes, and were briskly moving towards the gate.

An older man, perhaps the father, had joined them, all agog to know what the buzz was. Lance pulled off his hoodie and shook his head. His eyes were on the young woman — and hers, it seemed, were on his brilliant blue eyes and blond buzz-cut hair.

The older woman spoke up. "Calm down, major, let's not make a scene here." She tugged the younger woman's arm.

"Come on, Augusta, let's get to our seats before the crowds begin."

Augusta Curtis Carnegie was a dazzling product of upper-crust Chevy Chase, an obscenely wealthy Maryland suburb just outside of Washington, D.C. The only child of a United States ambassador to Great Britain and a runner-up Miss America contestant from Charleston, South Carolina, Augusta had grown up in a swirl of social climbing hypocrisy — high-brow cocktail parties, political fund-raisers and charity auctions.

The marriages she had observed seemed shallow and opportunistic. Infidelity was seen as business as usual.

Meaningful, unfiltered and honest conversation ran at a minimum. Augusta fully intended to escape this toxic environment before she was irreversibly influenced by it.

Miss Porter's Private College Preparatory School for Girls seemed like an appropriate solution. A prestigious New England boarding school with a hefty price tag, established in 1843, it had all the bourgeois trimmings necessary to polish up a sensible, ambitious young lady. And it did. Augusta thrived on the academic stimulation and was one of the better members of the swim team.

The absence of male company did not bother her. She excelled academically and athletically without distraction. When it came time to choose a suitable college, she picked Vassar. Her parents, Octavia and Horace, agreed to the all-girls Ivy League choice despite the high tuition fees.

When Octavia had mentioned the football game in their last obligatory Sunday afternoon phone chat, Augusta had not been pleased. "Must I, mother?" she had whined. "You know I detest football! And Major Sedgwick is such a monstrous bore!"

"But Augusta, darling, this is a great opportunity. Four front row seats right on the 50-yard line. And Sedgwick was such a dear to secure them. God only knows whom he had to bribe. Sitting next to him for three hours won't destroy you, you know. He's not all that bad. Plus you'll get to spend some special time with Daddy and me! You'll love it!"

Sensing her daughter's pout, Octavia pushed on, "You do understand the importance of this particular game, don't you? It's classic Americana. It's Thanksgiving. And it's Army versus Navy!"

All Augusta knew from past experience was that football typically spoiled an entire Thanksgiving afternoon. A bunch of loud, inebriated men clustered around the TV while the women did all the work.

"And I'm sure you've heard of Lance Allworthy. He's supposed to be a superstar! And a looker too!"

Remarkably, even Augusta had heard of him though she had no idea what he looked like. Indeed, considered possibly the greatest college football player in the history of the game, every sports announcer from every network that mattered had been touting Lance's extraordinary talents for weeks.

Octavia wrapped up the conversation, "Well, Miss Carnegie, that's that then, we shall see you soon. Be sure to look your best. The TV cameras will be right next to where our seats are."

Game On

The incident in the parking lot was well out of Augusta's mind by the time they found their seats, nicely positioned in the front row bleacher on the 50-yard line. After dutifully standing for the National Anthem as the Army's Golden Knights roared over the stadium to signal the start of the game, she sat down trying to keep as much distance between herself and Sedgwick as possible. But when her parents sat down, contact with him became unavoidable and Sedgwick relished it. Inspired by fantasy, he had choreographed this occasion down to the minutest detail. His white uniform impeccable and shoes so buffed that they glinted in the sunlight. He had no idea that the heavy splash of cologne he believed would attract Augusta to him was nauseating her.

The rival teams both marched the field for touchdowns in the first two quarters. At the half, the game was a tense 14-14 tie. Switching on what he hoped was top-brass charm, Sedgwick turned to Augusta. "I bring my own special concoction, non-alcoholic of course, and hot dogs don't agree with me, but I would be delighted to bring you a refreshment." He reached for her hand in the hope of an appreciative squeeze.

"I will pass," responded Augusta coolly, ignoring the outstretched hand. The thought of a hot dog brought on another green wave of nausea and intensified her throbbing headache. Apparently her lack of enthusiasm did not register with Sedgwick as he cheered and clapped when the halftime cheerleaders performed right in front of them.

The crowd roared louder. It sounded like the band had doubled its volume. Augusta felt herself vibrating to the repetitive thud of the base drum which by now had induced a full-blown migraine. *Oh Lord, give me strength.*

The second half of the game was everything avid fans could have hoped for. Having already thrown two touchdowns in the first half, Lance threw three more in the second half, breaking an Army quarterback scoring record. Navy, however, had answered each touchdown with its own strong pass-run offensive performance. With eight seconds on the clock Navy had the lead, the score 34-35, Army having missed an extra point. Army had the ball on Navy's 40-yard line, out of range for a field goal.

Lance signaled to the referee for Army's last time out. Observing the huddle, it was apparent that Lance was giving specific instructions to each player. His gridiron leadership on the field was without dispute as the team clapped in unison and broke into formation.

Pumping up the suspense, the sports commentators worked the crowd over the public address system. "What will Allworthy do?"

Lance took the snap and swept to his left. The Navy defense swarmed toward him, breaking through Army's tired front line. He faked a pass to the left corner of the end zone with a wave of defensive arms about to engulf him. At the very last moment, he ducked and peeled out from under the smothering mass of defensive players. He spotted an offensive receiver across the field in full stride heading for the corner of the opposite end zone. The crowd was on its feet as Lance set and fired a strike across the entire width of the field to the receiver in the end zone — just as the clock ran out.

The entire Army bench and coaching personnel stormed the field in celebration. There was joyous pandemonium as the Army players lifted their star quarterback on their shoulders and paraded him around the stadium. Having removed his helmet, Lance raised his right arm and punched the sky to punctuate the victory. His sweat-streaked blond hair framed a face that had triumph written all over it. The packed stadium of Army fans ate it up.

Meanwhile, Major Sedgwick had dropped his beet juice concoction all over his pristine white breeches. "Oh, no!" he yelped, jumping up, frantically trying to brush away the spreading crimson stain.

Augusta, now standing, could not take her eyes off the newly crowned king of West Point football. Even through the haze of her migraine, she recognized the blue-eyed young man they had seen earlier in the parking lot.

She momentarily turned toward Sedgwick, who looked like he had just been shot in the crotch. "Oh, do shush up!"

She then stared back at Lance Allworthy as he passed directly in front of her. She could have sworn his eyes stayed locked on hers even as the mob carried him forward. He swiveled his head, turning deliberately to maintain eye contact with her, an enigmatic smile on his face.

Wonder if I'll ever see him again, Augusta wondered.

Beirut, Lebanon

1977

Penthouse View

The soft loungers of the Penthouse Suite of Beirut's Hotel Albergo encouraged sleep. But Monsieur Henri Duchamp resisted the temptation to nap despite the strong possibility that a long night of pleasure lay ahead — once Karima arrived, of course. Instead, he opened the European edition of The New York Times and scanned the front page headlines and the foreign news highlights before turning to the weekly drama of European soccer. As his finger moved down the score column, he noticed an article off to the side about American football, a sport he privately felt could never compete with the sheer excitement and athletic showmanship of European soccer. His eyes fixed on the headline, *Voted Best Quarterback Ever*.

Henri cruised the article below quickly and then leaned

back, eyes closed. Another instant American hero. A moment later, he'd forgotten all about Lance Allworthy, distracted by the distant rat-a-tat-tat of gunfire. After two years of civil war, by 1977 skirmishes in downtown Beirut had become commonplace, a bizarre background music to which Henri had sadly become accustomed. Once the jewel of the Mediterranean, Lebanon had now become a white-hot crucible that pitted the ruling Maronite Christian government against an increasingly resentful Muslim population. The result was a domestic conflict marked by killing, destruction and instability, with no end in sight. Changing demographics and the fight for political representation had fomented confrontations everywhere.

Henri had once known and admired Lebanon as a civilized, multi-sectarian society with majorities of Sunni Muslims and Christians in the coastal cities and Shia Muslims in the south and the east. But now the influence of elite Maronite Christians on the government of Lebanon was undeniable and the cause of growing resentment. Being a citizen of France, the country that had colonized Lebanon, Henri Duchamp had unthinkingly sided with the largely Christian rulership. The growing Muslim population openly opposed the pro-western government.

In the middle of the brutal chaos, small Muslim resistance groups were forming, with names like the Lebanese Front, the Army of Free Lebanon and the Lebanese National Movement. To Henri, it certainly did not look like a conflict winding down. There was more to come and worse to come.

He put down the newspaper and looked west through the window of his suite, noting the traffic moving easily along Damascus Boulevard which split Beirut down the middle. Buses still ran north and south in and out of the city every two hours barring an accident or a breakdown. The bus-stop for his hotel was just three blocks away.

He hoped one of those buses was close and bringing Karima to him. Hotel Albergo, once a nobleman's mansion in the Akrafich Quarter but now a landmark, was as safe as one could hope for. He and Karima had met here many times without difficulty. Henri had reasoned that being located next to the large historic Jewish cemetery to the north and the Roman archeological ruins to the west would provide Hotel Albergo a measure of protection against hostile fire. His suite, replete with its own private pool with a starry sky view after sunset, looked down on a still peaceful courtyard filled with songbirds and fragrant jasmine.

He checked his watch and realized he was both hungry and thirsty. He had booked a dinner table for two at the French restaurant on the first floor. The French country food at Albergo's was excellent and he and Karima had always enjoyed it.

He looked at his watch again, worried. Any darker and it would not be safe for walking.

His thoughts turned to when they had first met four years ago at an academic awards dinner to honor outstanding Lebanese high school scholars. As French Cultural Attaché to Lebanon, he was to present Miss Karima Salmady with an award for Excellence in French. Although fifteen years older than she, he found this spirited but unassuming young woman who so effortlessly coupled brilliance with beauty instantly fascinating. What began as a combination of protective paternalism and benign intrigue had evolved over time into something much more.

Much more complicated. Henri's intense feelings towards Karima, who had grown up as a westernized Sunni Muslim in the Masraa district of northwestern Beirut, had made him sharply aware of his own mixed heritage, equal parts Christian and Muslim. He had presented himself to her as Christian, choosing not to admit his Muslim ancestry.

Henri's religious upbringing had not been simple. His father, from a mountainous part of the island of Cyprus, 150 miles west of Beirut, was a practicing Maronite Christian, an Eastern Orthodox Catholic denomination. His mother, from a wealthy Sunni neighborhood in northwestern Beirut, had been a devout Muslim. The two had met on holiday in the celebratory months after World War II when Beirut had been a picturesque seaside resort jutting out into the sapphire Mediterranean. Despite their religious differences, they had married and settled into the

Christian community in eastern Beirut, where Henri had grown up. Both had passed away naturally before the civil war broke out.

But now, with the inner conflict between the two religions he had inherited and his feelings for a young Muslim girl, his head burned with questions.

Where do I belong?

Is the Holy Father my true God or must I pray to Allah?

His soul wandered in search of an identity where he could follow his faith, whatever it was, with comfort and certainty. For now he remained lost in a private wilderness of conflicting forces. Indeed, not only did Henri struggle with the tragedy of the civil war raging outside but he also anguished over the implications of his own heritage. What would his dual faiths mean to Karima?

And why was she not here yet?

A Girl In A Hurry

Her heart fluttered. Hearing the day's fifth call to prayer, Karima Salmady knew she was running late. The dilapidated bus station was four blocks away. She hurried past the stalls lining the old city marketplace, wearing a black traditional, long-hooded *abaya* that covered her entire body except for her hands and part of her face. This outer Muslim garment was supposed to symbolize modesty and discretion but even concealed thus, Karima projected an undeniable sensuality.

Early that morning, in preparation for her upcoming evening with Henri, she had slipped on a silk chemise with a jeweled sash that lay completely hidden beneath her black overgarment. She had packed a few additional items, knowing that Henri would expect her to spend the night. She had brought no makeup but for a small tube of lipstick; the quintessential beauty of her subtle Arabic facial features required little or no assistance. A perfume Henri was partial to, a bathing suit, shorts, a silk blouse and slacks and a pair of Gucci sunglasses were all she needed. She had tucked inside her bra a small purse containing two 50 piastres coins, knowing her only expenses would be the bus fares to his hotel and for the return trip home.

Karima had spent the first part of the day working at her father's pharmacy on Hamra Street. Once it had been the go-to pharmacy for locals and tourists. At 22, Karima was especially useful to her father's business because of her fluency in French, English and several of the more common Arabic dialects.

By Lebanon's standards, Karima was middle class. Her father, Hassan Salmady, was a shrewd and intense self-made Muslim who had left his daughter's upbringing to his emotionally distant but traditionally subservient wife, Madalena. Early in her marriage to Hassan, it had become clear that her relationship with him was less about love than it was about escaping from her overbearing older sisters and her strong desire for motherhood. Witnessing the growing coolness separating her parents, Karima questioned the practice of arranged marriages and frequently wondered if she herself would ever experience a relationship based on genuine love. Whatever that was.

She had never quite understood the actual nature of her father's work and often wondered if some aspects of it were not completely aboveboard. Matters had grown even more murky since the civil war had broken out. There were hushed meetings behind closed doors in the back room of the pharmacy, attended by grim-looking men, never more than four or five. Once Karima had pressed her ear to the door but the murmurs within had been too low to be understood.

Then there were the crates. Some evenings she would see collections of long boxes outside the backroom; by evening they would have disappeared. From time to time, large packages would arrive which her father would place inside a giant vault at the back of the room.

One thing was already clear to Karima — the pharmacy was not her future. She was a gifted young woman who sensed her potential for a better life. With her mother's encouragement, she took a broad range of courses at the Arab University of Beirut, within walking distance from her home. For two years she studied French, languages of the Ottoman Empire, the History of Islam, and conversational English. One day, she hoped, she would break through the parochial boundaries of her Beirut life to a postgraduate degree, perhaps in Paris.

The dust-covered bus shuddered to a stop. Karima dropped the fare into the slotted tin box next to the driver and made her way to a window seat by the rear exit. Just in case. The bus continued its journey, rattling and snorting through the crowded streets of downtown Beirut. Karima wondered if the driver found amusement in trying to run over as many pot-holes as he could. She wrapped her woolen cloak more tightly around herself and pulled down the hood to cover more of her face.

The weather had quickly turned cool and penetrating, with the dampness from the sea adding an extra layer of misery to the darkening gloom outside. The window, opaque with grime, shook as if it were about to shatter as the bus navigated the washboard side-street before turning onto the once-elegant boulevard Omar du Lac that ran three blocks east of the glitzy hotels district that was now a war zone.

The magnificent hotels that had once stood as icons of Lebanon's thriving tourism industry had taken a battering over the past two years. For the Muslim and Christian forc-es locked in combat, the upper floors of centrally-located hotels offered the strategic advantage of elevation and over-view to whoever occupied them. The hotels that received this unwelcome attention from the fighting forces paid a heavy price. Among these was the brand new, 30-story Holiday Inn, regarded as a sniper's haven because of its height. Once the grandest of hotels for dignitaries, diplomats, local re-porters and foreign correspondents, it was now a devastated, empty shell, its windows broken, its façade pockmarked by the steady bombardment from both Muslim and Christian forces battling for the tactical high ground.

The bus entered Martyrs Square, easing past the statues of nationalists who had given their lives fighting for Lebanon's freedom from the 600-year rule of the Ottoman emperors. It always amazed Karima to think that at one time the Ottomans had reigned over an area that was now occupied by 13 countries in southeast Europe, West Asia and North Africa.

The sounds of distant gunfire receded as the bus entered Damascus Highway, picking up speed. Karima dozed off for a few minutes before she was jolted awake as the bus ground to a halt at the corner of El Inglizi Street.

Karima felt the evening chill as soon as she stepped down onto the sidewalk. The ground floor French bistro at Hotel Albergo was just three short blocks away. Minutes later she was in the cozy warmth of the foyer. An immediate right turn brought her to the door designated *Mademoiselles*.

Within, she removed her cloak and neatly folded her monastic outer garment, putting it away in her roomy shoulder bag. Turning to the mirror, she tucked a few wayward hairs back in place and applied a touch of lipstick that would no doubt soon find itself on Henri's cheek. A string of pearls complemented her tailored silk chemise.

You only live once.

Á La Carte

"Ah, mademoiselle, you are finally here!" There was no mistaking the relief in Henri's voice as he stood up. "How *merveilleux* to see you!"

"The pleasure is, of course, all mine, Monsieur Duchamp," Karima said as she pecked him on the cheek and then slid into her chair, allowing the chivalrous gentleman almost old enough to be her father to gently push it in.

The familiar, soft-lit ambience of the quaint speakeasy French restaurant welcomed them like an old friend. Their meetings always started this way, with a formal flourish. Karima knew all eyes were on them and that those watching were busily fabricating fantasies about who they were. The romantically toned and highly audible banter continued between them until the starched waiter arrived bearing a chilled carafe of a fine Bekaa Valley Chardonnay. Glasses were filled. With a little help from Henri, Karima had easily outgrown any Muslim inhibitions about consuming alcohol.

"Your favorite, my trinket," Henri said, raising the goblet, his voice now lower and more seductive.

"You do know how to please a woman, don't you, monsieur?" she said softly, equally affectionate.

They turned their attention to the menu. The fish was always fresh, caught each morning by local fishermen. They settled on flounder and prawn almandine, which blended nicely with the amorous conversation that danced easily between French, Arabic and English.

The mood shifted subtly after dinner. As if they had been gently reminded of reality, the pleasantries trailed off.

Karima's voice was gentle when she spoke, reaching for Henri's hand. "Something burdens you and I can't tell what."

Henri shrugged in a cavalier way, trying to make light of the question.

"The war?" she questioned, refusing to be sidetracked.

"We live in confusing and dangerous times indeed, my sweet. When will it all end, I ask?"

Karima nodded but she knew Henri had cleverly dodged the question.

"You too are troubled," Henri said. "What are you not telling me?

Karima looked away, debating whether to tell him, what to tell him, how much to tell him. She did love and trust this man but they had not till now ever discussed family matters, neither his nor hers.

"In all this turmoil," she said, "my father baffles me."

Henri waited.

"He's been tense, he has many things on his mind. He has been increasingly distant and distracted lately. Sometimes it feels like he finds his family to be an intrusion into something much more important. He hardly even acknowledges my mother."

"Do you think it is the war? Or is it the marriage?"

Karima threw up her hands. "Their marriage seems so wrong. There is no joy or laughter. Each appears to be a victim of a set of rules they neither made nor can control."

Henri nodded. He had some insights into the Sharia law that governed Islamic life.

"I feel so sad for my mother," Karima said. "She suffers so, under the pressure of Muslim male domination."

Henri squeezed her hand. "And yet he seems different with you, does he not?"

"Yes. He so often looks the other way when it comes to my behavior."

"Yours – or ours?" Henri said, trying to lighten her spirits.

Karima gave him a wan smile. "Here we are. I disappear for a long weekend with you, coming home with color on my lips and perfume in my hair. I cannot believe my father wouldn't notice such things. He once heard me talking romantically to you on the phone, and Sharia law forbids that, but he never mentioned it at all."

Karima paused to consider something. "He knows I've been stealing birth control pills from the pharmacy's inventory. Do you know what happens to Muslim girls who lose their virginity before marriage? We're finished. We get disowned, invisible. Yet my father has said not a word."

Exasperated, Karima threw up her hands again, "He's almost complicit!"

Over strong coffee, they shared a dessert of baklava with pistachios steeped in rosewater syrup.

"I have special plans for us tomorrow, my sweet," Henri announced mysteriously.

His plans often stretched beyond her own imagination. "Soooo — how long must my curiosity wait, monsieur?"

They took the elevator to the penthouse. Henri poured two generous snifters and offered Karima one. He closed his eyes and took a sip of the Remy Martin Reserve before saying, too casually, "Tomorrow we go to Cyprus and spend a few days. The weather will be magnificent!"

The cognac had already fed Karima's glow of contentment. She threw her head back and let out a childish squeal.

"Oh, dear Henri! That is so perfect! That sounds like a to-the-moon-and-back idea to me, my prince!"

Cyprus Secrets

"We should be there around 10 am," the deeply tanned Greek captain announced. "Alfie will be waiting for you." He winked and a look passed between him and Henri.

The dawn sea breeze and the fresh scent of the Mediterranean wafted over them as the 40-foot World War II era Benetti cruiser motored across the stretch of water that would take them to Cyprus. Now a refurbished, privately owned luxury classic detailed with teak and pear wood, the boat's name had recently been changed from Vespucci to Eros. How appropriate, Karima thought as she climbed aboard, noting the gold lettering against the transom's varnished mahogany.

Soon they were navigating calm seas and open waters. The captain eased the twin throttles into cruising speed, the two six-cylinder diesel Volvo Pentas barely audible. Karima and Henri settled into a pair of comfy blue loungers on the private foredeck. Light, lazy conversation passed back and forth between them until Karima turned toward Henri and changed her tone, becoming softer.

"What are you thinking, Monsieur Duchamp?"

Henri looked distant, lost in another world.

"Where are you? Why so serious?"

Henri reached over and brushed a wave of Karima's glistening dark hair away from her cheek and found her hand with his.

"I am here, my sweet."

He squeezed her hand.

"Welcome back, my dear stranger. Your daydreaming leaves me all alone."

Breakfast was served, ending the conversation. In silence under the small shaded dining terrace, Henri and Karima relished the baked eggs with spinach, tangy sheep's milk yogurt and a savory pastry. It would hold them nicely until lunch.

Two hours later, the Eros docked in Larnaca's inner harbor. The two gathered their few belongings and disembarked. Henri was the first to spot his crimson 'friend'.

"Voila!" he called out. "Alfie!"

Henri had always admired the seductive, Italian elegance of the 'Rossa Red' Alfa Romeo Spider convertible. He was certain he had found the only one of its kind available for rent on the island. The eager high-compression V6 engine sounded ready for takeoff. The top was down as requested, Henri noted with satisfaction; as promised the weather was indeed perfect.

Henri tipped the captain generously as he opened the door for Karima, who had wrapped a flannel beach blanket around her shoulders and covered her head with a scarf. Henri reached over and buckled her in before fastening his own seat belt. He moved the gearshift into position, released the clutch and eased his turbo toy onto the street. The rear wheels chirped as he dropped into second gear, and they were on their way.

The mid-morning sunshine washed the countryside with a blaze of wildfire reds and yellows and every shade in between. Alfie confidently hugged the winding cypress-lined coastal road. Henri turned to Karima and attempted a schoolboy grin. Karima managed a half-smile back.

Heading northwest, they remained quiet for the first hour of the drive, each lost in their own thoughts. Karima's mind was full of questions about this man she had grown so close to. *Why is he so remote today? Where is he taking me? Who am I to him? Will this bond between us last? How will it end if it ends?*

The roadster sped along the southern foothills of the Trudoos mountains which divide Cyprus in two, the northern half primarily occupied by Turkish Sunni Muslims and the southern by Greek Christian Cypriots. Despite their religious differences, tensions between the two regions were not inclined towards violence. Henri had not felt there was any great risk in making the trip.

In his mind, he replayed the morning's headlines from The New York Times — Muslim gunmen take American hostages over the killing of Malcolm X. Indeed, 1977 had been a bad year for America, with the nuclear arms race, government shutdowns and a crashing stock market, to say nothing of an energy crisis and a deep recession. *Did America deserve this?* he wondered. Could it be heading towards self-destruction just as Lebanon seemed to be? How much of the blame belonged to the naked power and greed that seemed to characterize America's global presence? Perhaps this was what ideological suicide looked like. Perhaps it was time for America to be taught a lesson for throwing its imperial weight around the world. Henri shook his head. So many questions.

An hour later, he brought Alfie to a stop in front of a 17th century stone monastery partially hidden behind a grove of tall pine trees. A vegetable garden to one side and a sign declaring the time of the next service suggested that the simple structure was still an active place of worship.

They did not speak as Henri walked slowly around the building, Karima close behind. A low cast-iron fence defined the boundaries of a small cemetery. A latched gateway opened to let them in. The grass was manicured and the graves arrayed neatly in rows.

Henri came to a stop and lowered his head in front of two small moss-covered gravestones. Karima read the names on the headstones: to the right lay Pierre Gustave Duchamp, 1920-1963; to the left, engraved similarly, was the headstone of Aliyah Pasha, 1922-1965.

Karima looked down at the final resting places of Henri's parents. A man and a woman, both short-lived, born and dead within years of each other. One of them was Christian; the other could not have been.

"Your mother —?"

Henri nodded quickly before Karima could complete the question on her mind.

"Yes, she was Muslim."

Sunset To Dawn

They paused only briefly at a neighboring village to pick up lunch, consisting of a freshly baked baguette, a quarter pound of prosciutto and a generous wedge of brie, to be washed down with a bottle of fine Italian Pinot Grigio.

The sun was high in the sky when they approached Ayia Napa, location of their luxury seaside hotel for the night. The secret beaches there, with their mountainous backdrops, were considered among Cyprus's finest. Countless small lagoons and sea caves offered not only bright white sand and deep crystal water but also in many cases virtually complete privacy. Henri slowed Alfie down to a crawl, scrutinizing the hedgerow to his left.

"There!" he said, triumphantly pointing to an irregularity which Karima could now appreciate as well. Partially obscured by a tangle of dense bottlebrush was a crude gate consisting of two posts about six feet apart. Throwing a wink at Karima, he eased Alfie through the narrow opening.

"You devil you," said Karima flirtatiously. "I didn't realize you had these secret hideouts tucked away."

"The day's excitement has only just begun, my lovely mermaid!" Henri said mischievously.

He maneuvered Alfie carefully through the dense vegetation, bringing her to a stop several minutes later just off the narrow pathway. Ahead of them lay a wooded area, with a brightening just beyond. They walked down the woodland path, Karima now a willing accomplice in whatever mischief Henri had in mind.

The path ended and they were looking down a steep set of stairs crudely cut into the rock face. Far below was a small beach cloistered on both sides by high stone jetties, the water a warm transparent turquoise. A gathering of cypress trees provided some shade and enhanced the air of romantic seclusion.

Two lounge chairs were positioned facing the beach. Henri and Karima carefully descended the stairway. A quick look around revealed that they were the only people present. They set down the blanket at just the perfect spot and Karima removed her cover-up sarong, reaching up toward the cloudless sky with both hands and stretching luxuriously.

"The best beach ever!" she announced, dropping down on the blanket and adjusting the top of her bathing suit downward for a more comprehensive suntan.

"I thought you might like it," Henri said gallantly as he shucked off his shirt and stretched out beside her. Their fingers found each other and entwined as they soaked in the quiet peace and warm sunshine.

"It saddened me to see you so troubled this morning," Karima said. "I hadn't known."

"Known what?"

"That you carry both Muslim and Christian blood within you though your name is Duchamp."

"And now you know," Henri said.

"I can't imagine — the constant war that must rage inside your heart."

Henri waved Karima's comment away. He was clearly uncomfortable.

"Whose side are you on?" Karima probed.

"Must I choose?"

"You tell me — must you?"

"And if I chose Christian, what would happen to us?"

"This is not about us. I have already done many things my religion forbids."

Henri said nothing.

"And your mother — what did she choose?"

"She asked for a Christian burial," said Henri.

"What do you want?"

"I want you," said Henri, rolling over and enveloping Karima with his strong arms.

"You want the Muslim," giggled Karima.

Henri lapsed into a reflective moment. "I think you're right, you know. The more I see what Christians are doing to Muslims in Lebanon, the more I feel this. I do want the Muslim."

Henri squeezed her to him. "And especially this Muslim," he said, biting her shoulder softly. "I am absolutely famished."

"Ow," said Karima. "I can see that. But we must swim before we eat."

She stood up, quickly shedding the vestiges of her bikini. Without hesitation, Henri followed suit.

"Catch me if you can!" Karima, now naked, had a head-start as they dashed toward the water. Henri was close behind. Karima hit the water first and waded gracefully through it until it reached her waist. As she dove head-first into the gentle surf, she suddenly felt Henri's grip around her ankle. Relaxing, she smiled and let him pull her back to him, her body sliding beneath his. His arms encircled her, each hand finding its own soft and ample breast. They rocked and bobbed for a few sweet moments, Karima sensing Henri's growing arousal against her buttocks.

As if by mutual consent, they broke the spell together, rolling simultaneously onto their backs, allowing the water to buoy them up. Henri cast a sidelong look at her, his pulse quickening as he saw Karina's breasts emerge just above the water's surface, the late morning sunlight lighting up the beads of water on her skin.

"My, what a big appetite you have," Karima said cheekily, noting signs of a growing hunger further down his body.

Henri rolled to his side, momentarily embarrassed. "Can we lunch now?" he pleaded.

Back at their blanket and dry again, Henri poured out two glasses of wine while Karima assembled the sandwiches. Together, they made short work of their lunch, washing it down with sips of the fine Pinot. "This is heavenly," sighed Karima. "I could stay here forever."

"So could I," agreed Henri, before his expression turned more serious. "I wish I didn't have to go to Paris."

"You do?" asked Karima, pouting just a little. "You never said anything to me."

"I'm sorry, my sweet, my mind was on many other beautiful things. They have called me back for a few meetings."

"But we have time, don't we?" asked Karima.

"All the time in the world, *ma cherie*," he replied.

The afternoon passed quickly.

The libidinous chemistry that had been simmering between them since the previous evening's romantic dinner, followed by the mid-day nakedness at the beach, came to a boil that evening after dinner back in their room.

Henri lifted Karima's flimsy blouse over her head and

slid her loose-fitting shorts down over her hips, allowing them to drop to the floor. Swiftly, in like manner, Karima disrobed him even as his eager hands drew her up against him, skin on skin.

With growing urgency, they fell on the large bed, lips and fingers eagerly exploring their bare bodies. There was no time for niceties. Henri slid into Karima and they began to rock together slowly in unison, pace accelerating soon to a delicious, rhythmic crescendo which ended in an explosive finale – hers with a sustained whimper and his with a thunderous bellow as he spilled himself into her.

The following morning they dropped Alfie off at the marina. Eros and the journey back to the realities of Beirut awaited them but a rosy mood cocooned the lovers, shielding them for a while at least from the grimness and shadows of their war-torn destination. By the time they reached Henri's penthouse, they were exhausted.

"Wine?" Henri said.

"I'd love some."

They raised a toast to good times and better days.

Karima's eyes fell upon the *New York Times* Henri had left open on the table the evening before. She saw that he had circled a particular article.

"What's this?" she asked, picking up the paper.

"Only America's latest sports hero, Lance something or other," Henri said sarcastically. "Not just another arrogant football superstar, though. This fellow boasts that he's going to be the first ever college quarterback in America to finish up in the White House."

Karima quickly scanned the rest of the article. "Well, here it says that what he wants next is to be a Rhodes Scholar."

"The quarterback who becomes a Rhodes Scholar and then President of his country," said Henri shaking his head, "Only in America."

On The Rhodes

"**How could there possibly be** any question about my qualifications?" Lance asked. "I thought I'd be a shoo-in."

Colonel Lionel T. Staghorn, chairman of the West Point Rhodes Scholarship Selection Committee, was apologetic. "It would appear that your grades are the only problem. A GPA of 3.5 just isn't competitive."

The highly prestigious international Rhodes Scholar Program accepted 32 young Americans out of 2,900 applicants. The process was brutal, more than Lance in his third year at West Point had bargained for. The selection formula looked at academics, athletics, character and manhood (a measure of 'personal vigor'). Other requirements included a persuasive interview performance, at least six letters of recommendation, a handwritten personal statement, the ability to schmooze at a cocktail party and a GPA of 3.9 or better. A regional selection committee would review all prospective candidates — but only if they were first endorsed by the West Point Selection Committee.

"I wish I could be more optimistic," Colonel Staghorn said. Lance's expression soured, then his face darkened.

"There must be something you can do. A man in your position." The colonel turned aside, looking for something in a drawer, showing Lance his distinctive profile. Something about it was familiar.

"You're excused, Cadet Allworthy."

Lance persisted, knowing that his behavior bordered on insolence. "Has there ever been a finer quarterback, sir?

Colonel Staghorn raised his eyes and held Lance's for a long moment. Then he said, "Dis. Missed."

Lance offered a half-hearted salute, turning at the door to take one last look at the colonel.

Where have I seen this man before?

It was late that night when the answer came. The big game. The stadium's parking lot. The screams. The army officer groping a woman who was trying to fend him off. Her hair yanked back, her blouse untucked and pulled open.

Lance had been carrying his camera. He'd clicked off some photos. He was sure he still had them.

He was sure it was him.

The letter with enclosures, in a sealed brown envelope marked

CONFIDENTIAL, reached Colonel Staghorn's desk two days later.

Two 4" x 6" color prints fell out on his desk face up as he slit the envelope open. The enclosed letter was brief.

> *Memories are precious, sir. I have cherished these photos of you since I took them. It was a day I'll never forget, and now I know, neither will you.*
>
> *It was such a pleasure meeting you and your charming lady friend that day. I'm sure she's recovered her poise by now. One look at you, and I knew exactly what kind of officer and gentleman you were.*
>
> *I hope these photos will help you remember that great day.*
>
> *As for my Rhodes recommendation, that is entirely in your hands, sir. I'm sure you will do the right thing.*
>
> *With complete discretion, I remain,*
>
> *Cadet Lance Allworthy*

Colonel Staghorn pushed his bifocals up the bridge of his nose for better focus, studying the details of the photographs more closely. He looked away for a moment, his fingers tapping the desk.

Do the right thing. He reached for the phone and punched in a number.

Months later, 60 miles northwest of London, Oxford University welcomed the handsome, young Rhodes Scholar from West Point.

It could be argued that Lance's year at Oxford laid much of the groundwork for his subsequent political posturing. He was surrounded by left-leaning liberal academicians whose thinking intrigued him. After reading the Communist Manifesto and studying the lives and works of Marx and Lenin, he had been struck by the seductive appeal of certain aspects of socialism to the Russian and Chinese working classes. What a clever strategy for controlling the masses, he thought.

Oxford's loose tutorial system required a high level of self-discipline and independence. To study on his own timetable was a welcome change from the overbearing culture of West Point. In addition to his studies, Lance immediately chose to join the university's premier debate team to further polish his natural gift for oratory. His silver tongue and persuasive rhetoric had all the power and appeal of a messiah. The melodious baritone rumble easily captivated his audiences. His words, often more syllables than substance, flowed effortlessly and convincingly.

The months flew by. However, while taking full advantage of the university's many opportunities, Lance had dedicated little time to the research necessary to complete his graduation thesis. He knew he had neither the motivation nor the scholarship required to write something of merit, especially with time running out.

"How much?" Lance asked the bartender, who made most of his money running a bookie operation on the side. For a little extra, he had slyly revealed, he could get a decent thesis written by one of his freelancers.

"50 bob for me and 8 bob a page for the writer. Cash."

Lance grimaced.

"You can write your title here." The bartender pushed a pen and a slip of paper towards Lance.

The Art of Manipulating Public Opinion: Adolf Hitler vs Winston Churchill – A Comparative Analysis. Lance slowly wrote down the title he had thought up some hours earlier.

"I need about 100 pages."

"Quite clever," the bartender said, deftly pocketing the rolled wad of bills Lance handed him.

It took only two weeks for the writer to finish the job.

And so ended the young quarterback's year as a Rhodes Scholar. The United States and law school at Georgetown awaited, but not before he and three rowdy Oxford classmates took a few days off and crossed the channel to Paris.

For "cultural enrichment", they told anyone who asked.

Close Encounters

Their hotel stood at the base of Montmartre, the Bohemian quarter of the City of Love, teeming with cafés and the homes of countless legendary artists and literary icons from the likes of Pablo Picasso to F. Scott Fitzgerald.

Of more interest to Lance and his friends, however, was the entertainment district of Pigalle, within walking distance southwest of their hotel.

Standing unnoticed near the entrance to the rooftop bar, across the street from the famed Moulin Rouge cabaret, Henri Duchamp eyed the bird-thin man he had come to meet, nursing a cold beer at the bar. The call earlier that day had been brief and direct. "We believe you will find our proposition interesting, monsieur."

He was well dressed. His upper lip was clean-shaven with a bushy but meticulously groomed triangular beard falling over his black tie. His dark eyes moved efficiently around the room.

Henri came forward to sit next to the man, offering his hand in greeting. The man raised his palm towards his face instead and said, "*Salaam alaikum*, Monsieur Duchamp."

Henri automatically responded, "*Wa'alaikum salaam*." He had dressed formally in a tailored suit with a starched white shirt, gold cuff links and a dark silk tie. He ordered himself a Remy Martin Reserve.

The conversation proceeded with inconsequential, lightweight matters for a few minutes. The man had not introduced himself and clearly had no plan to do so. He took a long sip of his beer and looked straight up into Henri's eyes.

"So tell me, my brother," he said. "What matters to you? What difference are you making?"

"Who do you represent?" asked Henri, ignoring the question and coming straight to the point. "Let's start with that."

"I represent your brothers and sisters," said the man. "The ones you don't hear though you see them every day."

Henri took his first sip of the premium cognac and said, "Go on."

"Do you know of whom I speak?"

Henri didn't reply, knowing the man would explain

himself if he waited.

"Your Lebanon," the man said. "Your Lebanon is wounded. Your people are bleeding. You live within the devastation, seeing it every day."

"The Christians —" began Henri.

"Your Christians are taking over," the man said. Henri flinched at the way he said it.

"They are not my Christians," he said, defensively.

"Then they are the Christians who belong to the western powers, to America and France and Israel," the man said.

"It is a war," Henri said neutrally. "Someone will win, someone will lose."

"And where will you be? With the winners or the losers?" asked the man softly. "With the Christians — or the ones they are trying to crush?"

"I can't take sides," protested Henri. "You know I'm with the French consulate."

"But France has already chosen, my brother. And they have not chosen the oppressed. The Muslim world is being crushed under the heel of the west."

"What do you want?" asked Henri, taking another sip of his cognac to steady himself.

"We need you. We need your mind, your experience, your intelligence — your passion. We need your influence and your many contacts."

"To do what?"

"To change the equation," said the man. "A long war is just starting, and Lebanon is only the beginning. The enemy is armed and numerous. We have our beliefs, our will and most of all, the advantage of surprise."

"I will need time to think," said Henri.

"There's no hurry but don't be too long. This is the moment your life has brought you to. Choose with wisdom."

"Whose side are you on?" asked Henri.

Before the man could respond, the quiet atmosphere of the bar suddenly changed. Four raucous young men, clearly having the time of their life, staggered toward the table next to the bar. Henri recognized three of them as British from their accents. The fourth one, a strikingly good-looking blond, was wearing a West Point Football sweatshirt.

The young man shouted, to no one in particular, slurring slightly, "More champagne here!" He snapped his fingers at a passing waiter. "Hey, you, garçon! Did you hear me?"

A bottle of champagne with four glasses was quickly served. Loud toasts were raised, voices climbing higher.

"Sing it, Lance!" said one of the boys and the other three began to pound the table and chant, "We want Lance, we want Lance."

With a show of reluctance, the drunk young blond stood up, swaying, drooling. As Henri watched, he clambered up to stand on the table, knocking a glass down and spilling champagne. He cleared his throat and began singing, off key and loudly. "Oh say, can you see —"

As he massacred the American national anthem, his three friends joined in.

The bar had gone quiet in horror; all conversation had ceased. One of the boys, realizing that this wasn't going well, tugged at the singer's sleeve. He angrily shrugged him off but eventually stopped singing and climbed down.

At that moment, Henri recognized him. That quarterback. The one who wanted to sit in the Oval Office one day. That vain, arrogant, all-American hero. Lance something.

In the stunned silence of the next few moments, everyone heard Henri's voice, low but perfectly audible: "*Juste un connard yankee.*"

Just another American asshole.

Lance heard it too and didn't like the tone of it though he had no clue what it meant. Standing up again, he lurched toward the bar where Henri sat. "What was that? What did you say about me?" he demanded, spoiling for a fight.

"*Rien du tout, monsieur,*" Henri said. "Nothing at all. We were just admiring your marvelous voice."

Lance looked flummoxed, not exactly sure what to do next. "Well, in that case," he said finally, "good night."

"And to you," said Henri as the unsteady fellow turned and moved away. Then, surprising himself, Henri called out, "*Allah hu Akbar!*" The bearded man at his side, hand still around his mug of beer, smiled.

The night was still young. The hobbled Rhodes scholars,

loud, stumbling, still carousing, made their way toward an alley lined with red lights three blocks away. Each light dimly illuminated a partly open doorway framing a heavily made-up female. Her seductive body language left little doubt as to exactly what she was offering that evening.

Lance was the last to make a selection. The other three men, having quickly chosen, had disappeared behind different doors. Alone now in the alley, Lance picked hastily, a woman who looked deceptively young and perky from where he stood but much older as he approached her.

"*Tu veux, ma cherie?*" she asked him, making eyes.

"What's on the menu?" Lance asked her.

"*Je fais ta pipe alors?*" she asked, with a light laugh.

Lance gawped, understanding nothing. "*Oui, oui,*" he said, not sure what he was agreeing to.

Before he knew it, she had knelt down and was at work right there out in the open, unzipping him while swiftly unbuttoning her blouse with her other hand.

Her breasts were completely exposed now. As she reached for his arcing manhood, Lance looked down and savored her chesty feast. In a moment it was all too much for him. As she touched him, he erupted, shooting forth a salvo of semen across her bosom.

"*Merde!*" she swore, dabbing at herself and trying to pull her soiled blouse together. "*Je m'en fou!!*"

Lance stepped back, trousers around his ankles, off balance and ridiculous.

It was then that his eyes fell on the figure of a man standing under a streetlight at the head of the alley, watching the scene with a faint smile. The well-dressed fellow from the bar. The one who had said *Allah hu Akbar. Allah the King.*

Lance hiked up his pants and rushed headlong past the Frenchman, who stepped aside to let him pass, murmuring, "*Plus de chance la prochaine fois*, Mr. Quarterback."

Better luck next time.

Washington, D.C.

1979

Legal Challenge

The handsome, olive-skinned Pakistani professor of international law stalked the classroom, weaving between and around the desks, an effective strategy for keeping his students awake and on their toes. The sleeves of his white silk shirt were rolled up, their armpits ringed with sweat.

"Economic and trade agreements with many of the Middle Eastern countries historically have been fraught with difficulties, generally under a cloud of mutual suspicion, deception and bad faith, with the negotiating parties often showing no moral or social obligation to tell the truth. It's no wonder the region has been an international powder keg, a cauldron of distrust where America is often seen as the Great Satan fueling strife and agitation."

Lance raised his hand. "So how do you explain what

happened yesterday in Libya?"

The professor paused, not used to interruptions.

"I believe protesters burned the US embassy in Tripoli in retaliation for the so-called criminal American imperialist's support of the religious militants who seized the great mosque at Makkah. They sought the overthrow of the House of Saud. Hundreds have apparently died."

Lance raised his hand again.

"We can see you don't like America very much," he said, goading the professor. "But keeping your personal biases aside, what do you think about the Iran hostage situation?"

The professor smiled, refusing to take the bait. "Last month Muslim students took over the US Embassy in Tehran," he said equably. "They claimed it was a den of American spies who were interfering with Iran's internal affairs. I have nothing more to add to that."

"So — whose side are you on? Your own country of America, now that we've let you become a citizen — or the Muslim rebels?" Lance pressed.

The professor took a breath, marshaling his patience.

"It's complicated. Like all things geopolitical, you must see it as a loose balance, a strategic but fragile economic and political alliance. The United States gets the oil while certain countries like Saudi Arabia get money and access to sophisticated defense technology and arms. Inevitably, the US gets involved in defending its interests in the region and some of the poorer countries feel violated by what they see as a pollution of their culture by the West. Some feel strongly that America is getting the better of the deal — and therein lie the roots of the animosity."

"You didn't answer my question," insisted Lance. "Whose side are you on?"

"Young man, I have no horse in this race."

Georgetown University Law School is strategically located in the Northwest District of Washington, D.C., only steps away from the Capitol and the Supreme Court. Lance's already established position in the sports world and his status as a Rhodes Scholar had handily gained him admission into the first-year class of 576 students.

Much to his delight, the army's top brass had caved quietly to his unconventional suggestion of attending law school rather than serve in the military, the customary obligation of West Point graduates. Of course, Lance had had to play his allergy card to make the case that he was physically not fit to serve. The system rolled over and let itself be easily manipulated.

Curiously though not surprisingly, he had been able to sidestep the LSATs, usually a compulsory requirement. What's more, Lance's perceived desirability as a star student and gridiron hero had helped him land a hefty scholarship out of the law school's endowment of over $2 billion, escaping most of the $30,000 dollars yearly tuition.

He had chosen a one bedroom apartment within walking distance of the campus and immersed himself in the complex environment of Washington, D.C. and all that it had to offer an aspiring lawyer. He preferred living alone to avoid distractions; the thought of having a roommate or a girlfriend never entered his mind. Indeed, Lance embraced his choice of Georgetown Law, a liberal bastion of progressive thought. It certainly looked like it had chosen him as well.

Meanwhile, 85 miles away, a certain lovesick couple had been torn asunder for 26 months while pursuing their careers.

ET had successfully completed Officers Training School at Quantico, Virginia, and found himself commissioned as a Second Lieutenant to study Tactical Warfare and Surveillance Information Systems.

"I'd rather be part of an elite fighting force," he wrote to Kat. "The man you love is qualified to become a pilot and a specialist in aerial combat. That's what I want to do."

Kat had graduated after four years at the University of Maryland with a master's degree in special education studying autism spectrum disorders. "Every time I see those children, it breaks my heart again," she wrote.

Their daily letters typically did not contain much factual information, but rather mostly expressed in various ways the pain they each endured being so far apart.

So were the phone calls.

"Being with you every day is all I dream of. So make it happen — and that's an order, lieutenant."

"So are you now my commanding officer?"

"It's easier if you get used to it, mister."

They would have preferred more time to put their wedding plans together but the Navy's orders for ET would not wait. They settled on a Las Vegas ceremony, their only option if they wanted some sort of memorable event under such hurried circumstances.

"Sounds like a bargain to me," ET beamed. "You get all of me for $449 plus tips and tax."

"Such a deal!" Kat enthused. "Nothing like getting a high-quality guy on the cheap!"

The perky personal wedding concierge grinned and said, "A great choice. The Pure Bliss Package is our best-seller. One mile in the limo, 30 minutes in chapel B, up to 30 guests, an 18-flower bouquet and an 8 x 10 color photo of the two of you at the end of the ceremony."

"How much to kiss the bride?" ET asked mischievously.

Kat elbowed him to stop the foolishness and said to the concierge, "Sold."

Lance recognized his sister's calligraphic handwriting on the envelope as he opened it.

Katherine Allworthy

and

Earnest Thomas Haynes

Request the honor of your company

at their wedding.

on Saturday, 19th July 1980 at 2 PM
Chapel B
827 Las Vegas Blvd. South
Las Vegas, Nevada 89101

Lance looked put off. "How inconvenient," he muttered to himself. He instinctively disliked family gatherings but a part of him recognized that this was perhaps a little more than a family get-together. He recognized the value of ET as a chronicler — had he not so efficiently recorded Lance's every action and expression during high school? Better to keep such talent in one's corner, even if it meant enduring his sister's wedding.

Then there was the matter of Cleo, whom he loathed but also needed. She would surely be there and would surely 'bump' into him — and there would no doubt be sharp words, maybe even a scene. They might even ruin the wedding for everyone.

Then again, perhaps it wouldn't be such a bad thing to bump into her after all. It had been a while since he'd had his last allergy jab.

He folded the invitation and thrust it into his pocket.

Don't Drop The Bride

"You may kiss the bride."

ET moved aside the translucent veil covering Kat's face and whispered, "Do I need his permission to do this?"

Kat closed her eyes, cocked her head and whispered, "Not anymore, lieutenant."

The small gathering applauded the lengthy smooch. A few tears trickled from mascara-ed eyes; men smiled, some caught up in the moment as well.

The dinner after the wedding was at a quaint Italian restaurant a few blocks away. The group of close friends relished the intimate atmosphere, enjoying the opportunity to either catch up or share their stories of the "perfect couple".

After everyone had arrived, ET clinked his wine glass

and stood up. "Kat and I so appreciate your coming all the way to Las Vegas to celebrate our lifetime gamble with one another." He raised his glass, grinning. "Though I personally believe the odds of us living happily ever after are better than 50/50."

Cheers and stomps and hoorahs.

Kat winked at ET and stood up, raising her glass. "You can bet on that."

Lance watched, leaning against the bar as he waited for his cocktail to arrive. Cleo, puffing on a cigarette, walked past him, glaring, her pale color reflecting a life that had seen little sunshine both literally and figuratively. Her brown hair, short and simple, was low-maintenance and nondescript. Her redeeming features, if one looked, were her large blue-green eyes and a figure that boasted curves in all the right places. This evening, a rare touch of lipstick added a bit of pop to her face.

Lance couldn't resist provoking her.

"Hey, doctor pathologist, you know those cigs can kill you," he called out. "Any interesting dead bodies lately?"

Cleo stopped and replied without turning to face him. "Well, I guess you would know about dead bodies, wouldn't you? How is it working out for you with your ambo-chasing classes? Or should that be the fine art of the grocery store slip-and-fall?"

Lance realized this was not going well. Plus he couldn't afford to rub her up the wrong way this evening.

"Awww, sis," he crooned. "Don't be like that. It is your best friend and beloved sister's wedding, after all. We need to be good."

"Right," she said, taking a drag from her cigarette before snuffing it out. "As if you ever cared about anybody's wedding."

"Tell you what," Lance said. "Truce till next week. What do you say?"

"What happens next week?" asked Cleo with a scowl.

"I thought I'm seeing you for my spring season jab? No?"

"Nope, bro."

"I'm sure I told you," said Lance, feigning confusion. "You must have forgotten to ink it in."

"I don't forget such things."

"Awww, be a darling then, sister of mine — make a little room in your busy, busy schedule for your loving brother, won't you?"

"Oh, joy," Cleo said. "This is just what I needed to round off my week."

She turned to the bartender and ordered a Virgin Mary.

"Don't drop the bride!" shouted Kat.

"Wouldn't dream of it!"

But the attempt to carry Kat over the threshold of their Fountainview Suite at the five-star Bellagio Hotel and Casino was an epic failure as she, convulsed with laughter, tried clumsily to slip the gold-plated key into the slot.

The path of rose petals led directly to the bedroom and then toward the large free-standing soaking tub in the bathroom. Neither of them had ever seen such opulence. Kat and ET giggled as she emptied the container of bubble bath into the tub and rotated the gold-plated lever on the wall. Warm water came gushing into the tub through a porcelain port in the ceiling. The two returned to the bedroom and playfully helped each other out of their wedding attire. Moments later they returned to the bathroom, laughing hysterically.

The three-foot-tall tower of bubbles had engulfed the tub and Kat disappeared into the mound of suds. "Find me if you can!"

ET slid into the tub, his arms reaching for his bride hiding somewhere within the frothy castle. They gently washed each other and then stood up laughing once more, each now cloaked in a toga of white foam.

The evening was still young.

The next morning, ET's brain slowly emerged into consciousness, still dreaming of their delicious lovemaking the night before. He reached for the naked back of the woman lying next to him, his hand gliding over the swoop of her waistline and coming to rest on her firm buttock.

"Good morning, Mrs. Haynes."

With a familiar hum, Kat signaled him she was awakening. His hand traveled upward and reached around her, gathering in the soft warmth of her breasts and pulling her gently back against him. They remained motionless for several blissful minutes, their minds wandering in different directions.

How lucky I am to have found this wonderful man, Kat thought. ET's thoughts dwelt more amorously on arousing memories of the night before.

"And good morning to you, Lieutenant Haynes." Kat said. They kissed.

"Just wondering. Was there a money-back guarantee with that wedding package?"

"Nope," intoned ET. "Looks like you're stuck with me."

Kat nuzzled in. "Worth every penny."

Best Friends Forever

Three weeks later, the newlyweds settled into base housing at Reese Air Force Base in what seemed like the middle of nowhere, Lubbock, Texas.

"If you stand on a penny you can see Dallas hundreds of miles away," ET joked.

After Basic Officer's Training in Virginia, ET had opted for the highly selective and grueling Marine Corps Officers Pilot Program at Reese. It was also there that he met fellow officer Jack Goodwell. The rapport between them had been immediate. Twenty-two months of advanced aviator training passed quickly as they worked and learned together, mastering precision strike tactics, weapon delivery, air combat and surveillance maneuvering.

It certainly didn't hurt that they spent most of their

time in a spanking new F-4 two-seater Phantom fighter jet, an aeronautic beast with a top speed of 1,400 miles an hour. As their training progressed, it became clear that this two-man team was uniquely talented. Jack Goodwell, with somewhat superior reflexes and coordination, would be the primary aviator, while ET, with keener vision and expertise in photography and electronics, would sit behind the complex computerized surveillance equipment. Whom you chose to team up with while potentially in harm's way is usually the most critical decision for any new pilot and for Jack and ET it was a no-brainer.

"Plus our ladies get along so well," Jack noted wryly.

Kat and Jack Goodwell's wife Milly became fast friends, wearing earplugs while their husbands practiced supersonic aerobatics high above them. The Texas hiatus gave the couples almost two years of fun and fond memories.

Then Jack received his orders to report for active duty.

"Beirut, Lebanon, really!" he said. "Wouldn't exactly have been my first choice."

The good times ended with barely any notice, and Jack was gone. ET waited anxiously for almost a full month before receiving his own marching orders. He tore open the brown military envelope, breaking out in a smile as he read its contents.

By order of the Secretary of the United States Marine Corps, on August 1983 you will report to:

*Andrews Air Force Base for your pre-deployment
briefing and medical and dental clearance.*

*Once cleared you will be assigned to the
Marine Fighter Squadron in Beirut,
Lebanon, where you will be stationed for
one year starting 1 September 1983.*

As much as ET looked forward to working again with
his buddy Jack, a part of him regretted that his Texas honeymoon party was now over.

"Why Beirut?" Kat asked, worry in her voice.

"To keep the peace, I suppose," ET said.

"I don't like it," Kat said, shaking her head.

At 1600 hours, the lumbering C-130 touched down at Beirut International Airport and taxied toward the terminal on
the 10,000-foot runway flanking the cobalt blue Mediterranean. A man in military fatigues, standing beside an olive
drab vehicle, waited as the airplane finally came to a stop. Jack
Goodwell waved as his best friend descended the telescopic
gangway. The two men resisted a bear hug but saluted and
shook hands like two old buddies reuniting after years apart.

Jack threw the 60-lb duffel bag in the rear of the army
jeep as ET slid into the front seat.

"My ass is whipped, twelve hours in that thundering
monster, didn't catch a wink."

"Let's grab a brew and some chow, then you can hit
the sack. Our briefing with the base commander isn't until

0800 hours tomorrow."

As the first beers arrived, ET spoke. "This place sounds pretty nasty."

Jack nodded, "And scarier by the day. No one was happy with the Israelis invading southern Lebanon. It's led to a growing resistance movement from Syrian and Palestinian guerrillas, a really ruthless bunch."

"Last month's suicide bombing at the US embassy got us all pretty rattled stateside."

"The crazy guy drove right up to the front door and blew his ass up along with half the building."

ET took the last swig of his beer and signaled for another. "So what's in the cards for us here?"

"What we do best, my friend," replied Jack. "Fly low and take pictures."

"Of what?"

"The ebb and flow of warring Christians and Muslims."

"And how does taking photos help anyone?" ET asked.

"Who knows? Maybe we'll catch something that everyone else missed."

"So we're stuck in the middle of a street brawl until the bumbling diplomats in D.C. can figure things out?"

"Something like that."

The next morning Lieutenant Colonel Gunther seemed to have lost the muscles necessary to form a smile. "Ain't nothin' happy going on here," he growled. "Washington has no idea how vulnerable this damn place is."

He threw his hands up in the air, not caring if his words could be construed as insubordination. "We're sitting ducks, surrounded by militant Muslim guerrillas and an airport teeming with nonstop unidentified civilian traffic."

The room of young officers was silent. A freshly minted 2nd Lieutenant in the front row raised his hand, "What about some sandbags around this place?"

"Washington says that might look too aggressive. We're here as peacekeepers, remember."

"That's a load of bullshit," Jack spoke up, "Our carriers offshore are throwing naval gunfire and air attacks into Shia Muslim strongholds as we speak. I'd say Uncle Sam has already crossed the line."

Indeed, the chaos in southern Lebanon had taken its toll over the last twelve months. An Islamic Jihad organization had already taken responsibility for the bombing of the US embassy as part of Iran's revolution against "American and Israeli imperialism".

The Colonel directed his pointer to a spot on the map on the wall. "The war in the mountains southeast of Beirut rages, pitting us and the Christian Lebanese forces against a coalition of anti-government Muslim leftists backed by the Palestinian Liberation Organization and Syria."

He paused and waved his pointer toward Jack and ET. "You two are now the eyes of our mission, Operation Oversight. Your aerial views of the city and its surroundings will hopefully spot any serious enemy military activity. Your daily reports will go directly to the Lebanese government's defense ministry, myself and of course the commanding officer of the Israeli troops here. Your skillful surveillance may well end up saving a bunch of lives."

ET cast a wide-eyed look at Jack whose nose had wrinkled up as if he had just smelt a skunk. The commander did not notice.

"And that, gentleman, is that. Dismissed."

What Happened In Beirut

October 23, 1983. A light morning breeze wafted past the heavy steel gate fronting the four-story reinforced concrete marine barracks. The congressional inquiry would have questions to ask later about why, on that particular morning, the gates had been left open, and by whom. Within the barracks, some 300 men were stirring to life after the Sunday morning ration of extra sleep and the promise of a tasty three-egg cheese omelet and a stack of pancakes.

Nearly a mile above, Jack Goodwell eased back on the yoke of the F-4 Phantom, arcing a wide circle over Beirut. The peachy sun cracked the eastern skyline, illuminating the complex mosaic of dials and gauges before him. In the twin cockpit behind Jack's, ET engaged the camera's high-res 360-degree fisheye optics and looked at his computer screen.

"What a city!" he murmured.

And it was. A honeycomb of white-roofed multi-storied buildings mixed in with the few terracotta rooftops of private residences along the Mediterranean shoreline. Clearly visible on ET's monitor was a strip of black sand beaches with clusters of ocean-going vessels moored in inlets along the coast. Visible beyond was the international airport. Two decades earlier, Beirut had been considered the Paris of the Middle East. Its thousand-year-old ties to France had influenced its fine cuisine, architecture and bred a generation of fashionable and liberated women. Sadly now, civil war had repainted Beirut in somber, joyless new tones. Anxious faces and bulletproofed buildings dominated the urban landscape.

From a mile up, all seemed quiet. Jack took the plane lower for a better view of the airport and the blocky barracks building. He slowed the aircraft to 500 knots, just above stall speed. "Hate to wake these guys up so early on a Sunday morning," he muttered.

"Flying over a nude beach would be more interesting," ET added.

"God, I miss our girls!"

Directly below, a yellow Mercedes cargo truck had rolled up to the barracks, driven past the open gate and stopped in a clearing. ET spotted the bright yellow at once.

"What's going on here?" he asked.

Before Jack could answer, there was a blinding flash, followed in seconds by the boom of an explosion, creating a blast wave of compressed hot air that reached the plane, shaking it like a toy.

The first impact was followed by a thick cloud of black smoke which blossomed upwards and outwards, filling the air with debris and shards from the collapsing barracks below. The clouds darkened the air, reducing visibility to mere feet. Another shock wave of hot gas hit the aircraft, pushing it further upward.

"I'm losing control," shouted Jack.

The second blast came now, creating a new pressure wave of gas, smoke and heat.

"Damn it!" Jack roared, pulling back hard on the yoke but getting no traction. "We're going down, ET! Our hydraulics are fried!"

The jet fighter was spiraling downward at high-speed.

Jack once again attempted to engage the gyroscopic autopilot system. *Nothing.*

The altimeter flashed red. Altitude critical.

"Bail!" shouted Jack. "Do it now!"

Both men knew what a flawed ejection would mean — the risk of a vertebral compression fracture as 140 pounds of force was suddenly applied to the neck while almost all the blood was being sucked out of the brain.

"Jettison the canopies," Jack said, cool-headed in the thick of the crisis.

"You first."

ET extracted the IBM floppy disk from the surveillance camera and stuffed it into his pocket, drawing his elbows in tight before pulling the handle between his knees.

A thrust comparable to a 40 mm cannon shell ejected the rocket seats out of the plane. The parachutes opened three seconds later.

The two men floated to the ground, as helpless as a pair of spinning June bugs caught in the vortex of a ShopVac. ET hit the earth first, his parachute wrapping around him. Moments later the ground under him shook as the Phantom crashed and exploded just two miles to the north. It took several minutes before his clouded senses began to return. Where was Jack? Had he bailed in time? Is my leg broken? Who's going to get me out of here?

Twenty agonizing minutes passed before he heard the distant chop-chop of the Iroquois rescue helicopter.

"The largest non-nuclear explosion ever on this earth."

That was how Base Commander Gunther described it at the briefing the next day. There was gray ash everywhere. "The barracks was hit by 20,000 lbs of lethal explosives wrapped within canisters of flammable gas. We're still searching for bodies but at this point we know we've lost at least 180 American troops and over 50 French and Italian soldiers. The second explosion killed more than 40 French paratroopers inside the nine-story Drakkar building."

"Do we know exactly who had the balls and the know-how to pull this thing off ?" asked ET.

"The CIA is on it. It took some sophisticated planning. It might have been an inside job. The timing was precise and someone had left the gates wide open."

"What do you mean?" ET asked.

"We just don't know for sure at this point. But one thing is clear — a group of Muslim bad actors who call themselves the Islamic Jihad want us to mind our own business and get the hell out of Lebanon."

Jack Goodwell, left arm in a sling, wiped his brow and said, "No shit."

Made In China

Three years passed quickly before the young lawyer graduated from Georgetown Law. Having passed the bar to practice in the state of Virginia and the District of Columbia, Lance Allworthy elected to fulfill his military obligation by joining the Judge Advocate General's Corps on the North Grounds of the University of Virginia in Charlottesville. Better known as the JAG Corps, it was America's oldest law firm and one of its largest, consisting of 3,400 attorneys who served the various branches of the US military worldwide. Established in 1775 by George Washington, the JAG Corps boasted many famous cases including the treasonous Benedict Arnold and the co-conspirators behind President Lincoln's assassination.

Not only did Lance's legendary gridiron star status open

doors for him but his year as a Rhodes Scholar at Oxford and the three years at a high profile D.C. law school had given him an edge. He brought an academic halo and reputation that set him apart from other military lawyers. He looked forward to the next four years at the JAG Legal Center.

His grip on the intricacies of global political history also put him under a spotlight all his own. He presented arguments and debated cases with both rhetorical ease and an instinctive cunning that often mesmerized juries and opposing attorneys alike. While most of the legal cases in the military were mundane, involving such things as a young sergeant going AWOL or a brawl in the barracks over a smuggled six-pack, some required a higher level of sophistication. These generally were assigned to Lance.

The brawny Asian dressed in UPS brown, with mirrored shades obscuring much of his face, was waiting by the entrance to the JAG Corps gym. He had a delivery for one Lance Allworthy.

Lance took the large red shoe box and looked down at the Nike lettering.

"For you, my friend," said the courier. "With our compliments,"

"Your compliments?" Lance asked, perplexed.

But the man was gone.

Lance shrugged, entered the gym and proceeded to the

empty locker room. Within the box was a pair of expensive new Blazer Elite high-top workout shoes. He checked the label inside the shoe: Made in China. 11.5. His exact size.

He put the right sneaker on. Perfect.

His big toe hit something solid inside the left sneaker. He reached within and pulled out — of all things, a Chinese fortune cookie. Breaking it open, he read the message.

One who sees clearly sometimes knows it's better to look the other way.

Why was the shoebox so heavy? Lance pulled away the tissue paper lining the bottom. His eyes widened at what was revealed — a layer of neatly arranged hundred-dollar bills. A quick count established that it was about $10,000.

His new sneakers fit like a pair of custom-made gloves. Lance left the gym with a curious smile, wondering who in the world could possibly have bestowed him with such a gift and a load of cash. The answer would soon become clear.

The trial that began the next day was arguably Lance's highest profile case to date. It involved defending two army truck drivers accused of smuggling and diverting 50 kilos of the highly addictive synthetic opioid Fentanyl which had come into the United States from China. The truckers denied any wrongdoing, and after interviewing them, Lance took their case on, instinctively convinced of their innocence. More importantly, Lance saw the trial drawing broad media attention, given the damaging effects of this lethal and addictive drug.

And so it did. The trial played out under the full glare of the public gaze, and Lance emerged the shining star. As his investigation evolved, it seemed clear that the accused truck drivers had had no clue about the contents of the Chinese container they had delivered. They had merely been couriers.

The container had come off the ship in Newark, New Jersey and been driven straight to the army warehouse complex west of D.C. to be unloaded and inventoried. The container had been the specific responsibility of a procurement officer who oversaw inspections and distribution. The shipment, described as paper products, had come from Beijing. Eight tons of computer paper, three tons of army stationery with the D.C. letterhead, 300 pounds of envelopes and one ton of calendars for the upcoming year. The rest of the inventory consisted of a smaller number of pads, index cards and two 50-pound cartons of neatly packaged 4 x 8 inch ink blotters.

"In an age when no one uses fountain pens to write but rather ballpoints, it seems strange that this shipment would include over a hundred pounds of ink blotters," said Lance, looking straight at the jury. "More interesting is the fact that procurement officer Major Sloan was unable to account for the whereabouts of this curious portion of the shipment."

Lance continued, all eyes on him now. "Fentanyl is cheap and can be made on an industrial scale. China, where this shipment came from, is the major manufacturer. A speck of powdered high potency Fentanyl equaling a few grains of salt can kill an adult male. It comes diluted in forms such as pills, patches, lozenges and yes, even lollipops. This stuff is readily absorbed through the mucus membranes and the illicit drug culture which sadly surrounds us knows this."

Lance paused before throwing his final punch.

"And, I submit to you, so did Major Sloan. Those useless blotters were spiked with enough active Fentanyl to kill the entire population of Washington, D.C., and had an estimated street value of over four million dollars. Euphoria first, followed by addiction, or death by overdose can come quite quickly to those who suck on a small piece of this drug-infused blotting paper!"

No one was able to trace the 300-pound container of envelopes, an aspect of the trial that Lance conveniently chose to overlook. It wasn't until two months later that several envelopes were discovered during a random drug bust in Newark. Licking the adhesive on the flap would yield an instant Fentanyl high.

A gift-wrapped box just large enough for a pair of earrings sat on Lance's desk when he reached his office two days after the trial. He pulled at the ribbon and tore away the shiny paper, popping open the plush velvet box.

This time, the fortune cookie read: *Sometimes he who looks the other way finds unexpected gold.*

No one was surprised by the public appetite for Lance's

brand of legal theater. After the Fentanyl trial, the All-worthy name was hailed as belonging to not only a former sports hero but also an able legal warrior who had success-fully battled against the scourge of illegal drug trafficking.

Two months later, Lance was discharged from the JAG Corps, having fulfilled his military obligations. He wasted no time turning his sights to the task of finding employment, eager to affiliate himself with a high-profile D.C. law firm to advance his agenda.

The four distinguished-looking attorneys sat around the large conference table. Lance sat at one end, in a dark suit, conservative striped tie and shiny black wing-tips. The white-haired senior partner made the offer. "We believe you would be a perfect fit, Mr Allworthy. We are willing to pay you handsomely if you elect to join us. Our clients reward us royally for our specialized services."

"Specialized services?" Lance asked.

The senior partner leaned in and lowered his voice as if conveying a secret. "Important people always have ene-mies. We offer our specialized services to such high-profile individuals who might need protection from slander and unwanted harassment from the media."

Lance simply nodded. He understood perfectly.

The Law Firm

"I'm coming," **Cleo** **responded with** annoyance. I should make the bum wait a while, she thought to herself. The syringe now ready, she opened the door of her apartment and stood back.

"I'm in a hurry, Sis," Lance barked, as he pushed his way through the doorway, rolling up his sleeve at the same time. "Gotta get back to the office." As always, he stiffened and grimaced as Cleo plunged the needle into his deltoid.

"What would people say if they knew you were such a wimp?" she poked.

"I've always known that my dear sister could keep a secret. As can I. Sometimes," Lance replied, rolling down his sleeve. He seemed immune to the embarrassment another male might have felt at being exposed as a sissy. Placing his hand on the doorknob to signal his departure, Lance changed the subject.

"I see you got the invitation," he said, referring to the embossed, scripted card on her desk.

Cleo nodded and picked it up and began reading from it mockingly. "It is with great pleasure that the law firm of Hillars, Jefferson, Jabbar and Menendez proudly announces that Lance Allworthy has recently become an associate at our Washington, D.C. office. We request your attendance at a reception in his honor. . ."

But her brother had already disappeared down the hallway. Cleo had researched the company out of curiosity and had bad vibes about it. Behind a façade of professional respectability, the firm had made its fortune discreetly feeding off the bottom of the D.C. cesspool of sleazy, well-heeled public figures. Its *modus operandi* was to follow the money, like a vulture cruising for dead meat. Actual innocence or guilt mattered little. Deep pockets ran the show.

Whatever. Lance's career was of little interest to her. She turned and walked away from the door, stopping only to toss the invitation into the wastebasket.

It didn't take long for Lance to get comfortable weaseling wealthy well-connected people out of often self-inflicted trouble. The pickings were substantial, providing a wide-angle view into the web of American high society and the recognition that power and control often came with knowing other people's secrets. Lance became a master at the art of certain defense strategies. "Plausible deniability is my anthem," he once boasted. "And reasonable doubt is my secret sauce."

CASE 1: Anita Rodriguez, now 32, accuses Senator Josh Cornwallis (R), silent partner of Gentleman's Club of America, of touching her inappropriately 37 times and raping her 12 times over two years when she was a teenager.

Lance's secret sauce: "We must be compassionate. The girl was an illegal immigrant. Naturally, she lied about her age and would do literally anything to get a job. But she has withdrawn the charges, having realized that her future lies ahead of her. Senator Cornwallis does not hold it against her or her family. In fact, he has offered her parents a path to citizenship and jobs in a D.C. club."

CASE 2: The Department of Justice vs New Jersey Governor Antonin Fazzio, accused of gifting a car to the judge overseeing an IRS case against the Governor's son.

Lance's secret sauce: " Your Honor, we have documents that establish that the judge was a major shareholder and part owner of the very company that gifted him the car. It is absurd to describe this as a gift from anyone else."

CASE 3: Illinois Senator Corey Jackson (D) is charged with disclosing classified information to a Russian spy with whom he was having an illicit affair.

Lance's secret sauce: "We thought it best not to disclose that the young lady has been injecting meth into veins between her toes to avoid detection. As a recent immigrant, she was unemployed when she acquired a drug habit. It is entirely understandable that she would say or do anything to support her addiction. The documents will show you that Sen. Jackson has been like a father to her, trying to help her get her life back on track. I'm sure Russia would have a better choice in secret agents."

CASE 4: The Congressional Ethics Committee accuses Minnesota Congresswoman Cassandra Deerfield (D) of diverting campaign funds to her personal banking account.

Lance's secret sauce: "Your Honor, a woman in Ms. Deerfield's position has many powerful enemies. As you and I know, anyone can divert money into anyone's account to implicate them. Why, I daresay if Your Honor should find a windfall of, say a hundred thousand dollars in your bank account tomorrow — it would be no great feat to arrange it —"

It was all about who appeared and sounded right. The truth mattered not at all. But plastic justice did not come cheap and Lance's law firm benefited immensely from his efforts. Not only was he good for the firm financially but also it had become quite clear that his role now extended far beyond the brick and mortar of his office and the courtroom and had begun to insinuate itself into the political consciousness that surrounded the capital. He was indeed, to the unsuspecting eye, an emerging bright star.

Lance had sniffed blood and liked it. It was time for him to enter the wild and crazy game show of American politics.

Campaign Trail

Lance Allworthy hit the Virginia and D.C. political scene with the force of a tsunami.

After only a year and a half with a palpable groundswell of Democrat support at the age of 32, he began seriously considering a run for governor. His personal magnetism had already attracted a team of savvy, well-connected individuals who accurately recognized this shining star's potential trajectory and decided that when his political rocket took off, they wanted to be on it.

His words were filled with promise and intention, and reflected, to a substantial section of the population, a rising tide of optimism. Free healthcare, free daycare, free public college, clean energy, lower taxes and an increase in the minimum wage. The list went on and on.

His Santa Claus platform had almost universal left-wing appeal, especially because it included the assurance that the federal government would be footing the bill for most of these 'humanitarian' proposals.

With one year left of his four-year term, Virginia's current Republican Governor, Hyman Dolesse, had proven disappointing. He was inarticulate, dull and ineffectual, swaying passively in whatever political direction offered the least resistance. Those within Lance's inner circle of Democrat supporters recognized the governor's obvious shortcomings and saw a ripe opportunity for their candidate to be his successor.

To launch the campaign, Lance's political strategists advised a highly visible event to kick off his gubernatorial run. Lance concurred, envisioning a conspicuous town-hall-type gathering. Ample funding materialized from sources unknown, no doubt with strings quietly attached.

Rosslyn, Virginia seemed the ideal venue. Located just across the Potomac with a view of the Washington Monument and the capital, it hummed with undeniable political largesse. A high-income, densely populated metropolis, it contained enough movers and shakers who could, if they chose, promote a candidate they perceived as a winner and an advocate of their liberal political agenda.

The Marriott International was chosen as the perfect spot. The top floor consisted of a huge ballroom able to accommodate 400 people around 30 circular tables, a stage, a podium, an excellent speaker system and a phalanx of large doors which opened up to a spacious deck where people could enjoy the open air and a spectacular, panoramic view of the cradle of American governance.

"Just perfect!" Lance murmured, as he reviewed the lengthy guest list of prominent Democrats, noted for their influence and net worth.

Indeed, the invitees to what now resembled a political rally more than a town-hall meeting were members of every ethnic group within Virginia as well as a broad swathe of politicos from within the Democratic National Committee. Lance had personally requested the presence of his two sisters as well as (not surprisingly) his brother-in-law, the now highly-regarded photographer Major ET Haynes, retired US Marine.

There was just one thing not quite perfect about all of this. It was an uneasy thought that surfaced into Lance's consciousness from time to time as his political career had gained momentum. He instinctively sensed that the picture was incomplete. Something was missing, a necessary component of the political package he needed to present to the American people. Someone was missing. The perfect candidate needed the perfect woman by his side.

Odd, therefore, that thoughts of a wife should cause some unsettling twinges of ambivalence in him.

The political rally could be deemed a roaring success judging by the media attention and tabloid gossip it generated. The crowd of Virginia and D.C. glitterati was resoundingly supportive, giving Lance the clear sense he had whatever it took to ride the wave to the governorship of Virginia. The exquisite food and the copious amounts of alcohol no doubt contributed to the high spirits and optimism.

There were a few moments that could be termed either troubling or thrilling. As expected, ET and Kat were seated at the table closest to the podium so ET would have the best angle for photographs. The surprise was Cleo's presence next to them. Though Lance had included her in the invitation list, he had not really expected her to show up. Of late, she had been openly reluctant to attend any of his public activities. Her only limited contact with him had been when she grudgingly gave him his anti-allergy shot.

What was equally unexpected, even flat out frightening, was what happened shortly after the all-American dessert of apple pie with vanilla ice cream was served. Most of the crowd had moved to the spacious deck outside to enjoy the warm, spring evening. Lance had begun working the large crowd when an enthusiastic supporter asked him to comment on his election prospects. Without warning, Lance broke out in a coughing, wheezing fit. He quickly moved back inside and sat down, trying to catch his breath and recover his equilibrium.

The cause of the sudden attack, Lance realized, had to

be pollen from the decorative potted pine trees positioned around the terrace. He also realized that skipping several of his shots during the winter, when he typically did not experience allergies, had not helped. Cleo had warned him about this.

This evening, luckily for Lance, Cleo was at hand and responded promptly to the emergency, providing Lance with a fast-acting, chewable antihistamine and an injection of epinephrine into his thigh right through his pants.

It was now, as Cleo tended to him, that Lance noticed a striking woman about his age coming towards them.

"Can I help?" she inquired with obvious concern, looking straight at Cleo. "Is he alright?"

Cleo paused in mid-injection to look up at the woman, smiling for the first time that evening. "He'll be alright," she said. "Just an allergic reaction to something in the air."

"But thanks for offering to help," Lance butted in, trying to divert the woman's attention from Cleo to himself. Something about her enchanted him.

"Yes, thank you," Cleo said, completing the injection.

"You're completely welcome, I'm sure," the woman replied graciously. "By the way, I'm Augusta Carnegie and I'm delighted to meet you both."

Lance rose from his chair and extended his hand.

"Charmed to meet you as well," he said, raising her hand to kiss it, except that she withdrew it before he could.

Their eyes engaged for a long moment before Augusta

spoke again, "Believe me, the pleasure has been all mine. You've not changed a bit, you know."

So they had met, and she remembered it. Try as he might, Lance drew a blank. Where had they seen each other before?

Lance reached across the candlelit table and with both hands gathered up those of the stunning woman before him. Finding Augusta Carnegie's address and phone number from the political rally guest list had been easy. The two had been spotted dating at least six times in the five weeks since then and the pace of their relationship showed no signs of slowing.

"When I saw you at the Marriott that day of the rally, I knew I'd seen you before. But it was a whole day of torture before it suddenly came to me. That Army-Navy football game! You were on the sidelines with your parents. And some weird army guy."

The delicious French meal and espresso were over. Lance and Augusta were still holding hands across the table, their gazes intensely locked on each other. This time, Lance raised her hand and kissed her fingertips.

"Who could ever forget that face?"

Augusta withdrew her hand from his grasp and laid it on top of his. "Your face isn't all that forgettable, you know."

For a moment, Lance was not sure how to take the double-edged compliment but he came back with, "Utterly enchanted, my dear."

"Well, it has been plastered all over Virginia!" Augusta said sarcastically while managing to stay affectionate. "And look — the media just can't leave you alone." A pack of hungry paparazzi were crowded outside the restaurant window, cameras trained on the couple's every move and expression.

"You don't seem to particularly mind their attention either, darling," said Lance dryly. "I get the sense you rather like it."

Augusta squeezed his hand and smiled.

Lance turned flirtatious. "So — do you think we'll be happy together?"

"I wouldn't doubt it."

If there ever was a formal proposal of marriage, this backhanded moment was probably the one that came closest to it.

"We make a pretty persuasive pair," Lance remarked.

"I guess we do show rather well," Augusta acknowledged. And thus did the two beautiful people bask in their own self-admiration.

"Did you notice, back at the rally — they almost didn't care what I was saying? They just stomped and cheered."

Lance had already arrived at a driving insight of the American politician's life — you could sway public opinion even if most of your audience had no clue what you were talking about. "Voters are lazy creatures," he said. "Most prefer a diet of melodic sound bites to a full course meal of responsible civic scholarship."

They left the restaurant hand in hand, sensing they needed each other to maximize their chances of reaching their dreams. They were greeted by a volley of flashing cameras, lights and questions. A small crowd of photographers had been waiting the entire evening to get a picture of this couple whose political track might well impact the course of America's future.

The headlines of the next edition of the *National Enquirer* screamed: *Virginia Governor Engaged!* Consistent with its reputation as a pulp rag notorious for hyperbole and inaccurate journalism, the article was a total misrepresentation and yet it was not far from the truth. Lance was not yet governor and he and Augusta were not yet engaged — but both events were already as good as true.

Six months later, Lance Allworthy became the Commonwealth of Virginia's youngest Governor. He and Augusta announced their engagement two days later, in a joint interview with *People* magazine.

Dearly Beloveds

And Daddy nailed down the Congressional for the rehearsal dinner and the reception," Octavia Carnegie gushed.

"Nothing but the best for the new gov'na and my daughter," Horace Carnegie enthused as he wrote yet another large check. "$2,500 a person should cover it."

Augusta had no idea where the money came from; she had been bred to never look at the right side of a menu. Her head swam, clueless about the nuts and bolts of planning a wedding of such blue-blooded magnitude. Her wedding. Her wedding with Governor Lance Allworthy.

Which should it be — Oscar de la Renta or Carolina Herrera for the wedding dress?

"Mother, I just can't decide."

"Well, at least we're settled on the menu. Caviar — Beluga of course — and a Kobe fillet with a Maine lobster tail."

"The guest list just keeps getting longer," Augusta said, not complaining. All this talk of delicacies was making her downright hungry.

"Mostly political royalty looking to rub shoulders."

"Not to mention, sip some top-shelf booze," Augusta added wryly.

"Won't Horace just be in heaven, holding court with all the town elites."

With you right beside him lapping up every second of it, Augusta thought uncharitably.

"D.C.'s St. Ann's Church agreed to a perfect 4 pm wedding service, Augusta dear. It's only eight short miles from the club."

Augusta wasn't sure exactly where God fit into her and Lance's life. She did recall Lance saying once, "Carrying a Bible into a church always looks good to the masses."

The rehearsal and the dinner that followed were impeccable. Kat raised an optimistic toast. Cleo fumed. Almost everyone else got drunk. ET took some candids using his miniature police detective camera designed primarily for espionage.

And thus they arrived at the day of a wedding that would be remembered for decades. Augusta finally went with the Herrera high-collared tulle skirt gown. Dazzling. Lance looked like a penguin.

"You will wear tails," Octavia had decreed. That was that.

The largest organ in D.C. blasted Wagner's processional over the heads of over 500 attendees who sat flanked by vast stained glass windows and towering biblical statuary. The vaulted ceiling reminded Augusta of Notre Dame. Cleo had her own views, of course. Classic evangelical theater laced with highbrow hypocrisy, she thought. Lance's specialty.

Virginia senator Roman Cavanaugh gave the toast, apologizing that the president couldn't make it. "Too busy running the country," he said, attempting wit. No one laughed.

Former football teammate Maxwell Donahue, now red-faced and obese, hoisted his refilled glass of Dom Perignon into the air and slurred, "Virginia is in good hands now. Here's to my old gridiron West Pointer."

Right on cue, the 23-piece orchestra played *Happy Days Are Here Again.* "Oh, please," said Cleo, feigning agony.

Many guests began to dance, while the bridesmaids opted to first refresh their makeup. The groomsmen retreated from the loud music to stand on the 18th green of one of the most prestigious golf courses in the world, lighting up complimentary Churchill Honduran cigars.

Select members of the press had received coveted passes to attend the political circus with all its flamboyant trimmings. The Greatest Show on Earth would be the next day's headline in a leading check-out lane tabloid. Video cameras rolled and flashbulbs popped amidst hyperbolic interviews.

"So, Governor, what's next after you get Virginia straightened out?" asked a pert reporter from CNN. "People are saying the Oval Office?"

Lance smiled, then chuckled. "Except that I don't like yellow walls."

"But you'd look great behind that Resolute desk, my dear," whispered Augusta, standing right next to him.

The fireworks were breathtaking. "Better than the 4th of July," said Horace as the band launched into a salute and a colorful bouquet of comets lit up the night sky.

Lance Allworthy and Augusta Carnegie were now official. "Langusta" was the portmanteau moniker awarded to the power couple by *The Washington Post* the next morning.

"I bet we could samba on the head of a pin!"

ET threw his tuxedo jacket on the back of the living room's welcoming easychair and collapsed into it. He let out a long sigh of relief, indicating he was glad the evening's exhausting event was over. Kat followed his lead, flopping herself into his lap at the same time, kicking off her high heels. She had known there would be dancing and she preferred to be a bit taller when she and ET swirled and swayed.

"Would Fred Astaire mind massaging my poor feet

back to life?"

"It would be my absolute pleasure."

They moved to the couch, and Kat stretched out, extending her feet towards her husband. His hands knew what to do. Kat closed her eyes and enjoyed his experienced touch.

"What a wedding!"

"A really big show!" ET chuckled, trying to mimic Ed Sullivan's famous line.

"Everybody who's anybody was there. Even dear Cleo showed up, looking rather fetching, I might add."

"It must have cost a bloody fortune," ET remarked, getting a pinch from Kat at once.

"More than our little chapel deal in Vegas, that's for sure. Right, cowboy?"

"Ours worked just as well, didn't it?"

"Did you get the feeling my brother is positioning himself to eventually run for president?"

"Sweetheart, I think your brother has been running for president since the day he was born!"

Springtime In Paris

Early spring in the City of Love never disappoints. As always, this time of year found Paris ripe and in heat. The warm morning air brought new energy to all manner of birds and blossoms. Paris was poised for romance.

As had been their custom, Henri had arranged a springtime Paris rendezvous with Karima. He arrived from Beirut late in the afternoon and took a rattly taxi to her flat. She greeted him with open arms.

"*Bon soir, mon chér*, you must be exhausted — and so very hungry. Dinner is almost ready."

While the spinach quiche warmed in the oven, they ate spring greens with vinaigrette and sipped a chilled Chardonnay. Karima noticed that Henri seemed subdued today.

"Monsieur Duchamp," she finally said. "Where are you?"

Seeming distant, Henri did not answer right away. Then he winked and offered her a half-hearted smile. "It's just been a long day, Miss Salmady. But I promise, I have only you on my mind."

"I see," Karima said. He rarely called her Miss Salmady. They finished dinner in silence, Karima cleared the table and then gave Henri a short peck on the cheek.

Among the many fine appointments of her flat were two spacious bedrooms each with a king-sized four-poster Baroque bed with satin sheets. Each suite came with a spacious luxurious bathroom equipped with a large walk-in granite shower chamber with six adjustable spray heads. The fragrance of fine Parisian soaps and emollients filled the air.

Karima slipped out of her clothes and stepped into the shower. She adjusted the jets and stood motionless allowing the warm water to cascade over her. She enjoyed the sensuous sensations for a while before reaching for the soap.

The shampoo came next and then the imported eucalyptus conditioner. After almost half an hour, she emerged from the shower and dried herself slowly before generously applying a fragrant body lotion. The lights were dim; barely audible music played in the background.

In her bare feet, wearing a knee-high satin robe, she

tip-toed across the hall to the door, slightly ajar, of Henri's bedroom. She could discern his silhouette on the bed. Henri's hair was damp and slicked back, after his own more abbreviated shower.

Letting her robe drop to the floor, she slid beneath the smooth sheets, drawing her warm body against his. She smiled in the darkness as she heard a familiar sound — Henri did not snore but often when he was sound asleep, he would purr, which Karima took to mean complete contentment.

Shall I disturb this sleeping giant? Karima asked herself as she laid her arm across his chest and spooned herself closer. Henri stirred and mumbled softly, "Welcome, *mon chou.*"

Without a word, Karima swung her leg over Henri's torso and straddled him, waiting to sense his awakening between her legs. Normally after a time apart, he was always eager to make love. But tonight felt different. Was he simply tired from his long trip? Or was it something more ominous?

She inhaled deeply, gathering in his clean, fresh scent and slowly began to rock her hips. There was no response from the man beneath her. Minutes later, with an exhalation, Henri dropped off into a deep slumber, leaving Karima suddenly and painfully alone.

It was some time before she drifted into her own sleep, crowded with chaotic dreams.

The next morning Henri greeted Karima with a mug of coffee.

"*Bon jour, ma petite*," he said, pushing the steaming brew towards her. Once again, Karima sensed his detachment from him. She took the mug and said, "I'm hungry."

At their favorite open-air café, only a block and a half away, they relished fresh orange juice and croissants.

"Such a beautiful day," Henri said, as they strolled arm in arm later under a canopy of blue sky and courting songbirds, kicking at small stones on the gravel pathway that bisected the flowering hedges of Luxembourg Gardens. They had been lovers for over fifteen years now and even though their meetings were intermittent, Henri had somehow always ensured that their relationship remained vibrant and intact. Why did today feel so different?

Henri cleared his throat and paused for a moment, his facial features tightening and his tone turning subliminally more serious. "The time has come for you to turn your life in a new direction, my treasure."

Karima looked up with some surprise at the man who had guided so much of her young life.

"Where on earth is this coming from, Monsieur Duchamp?"

"I mean it," he said. "I believe a new and more exciting adventure awaits you — in another country. One where you will make an indelible mark."

"I see," she said. "And I suppose you also know which

country that might be."

"Indeed I do, my sweet," said Henri. "Your next life will be in America."

Karima felt confused and unsettled. This felt like a Henri she had never met. At one level, she certainly had come to love him and trusted him implicitly. But he had also never asked such a big thing of her before.

Much of who she was today was thanks to Henri. After her two years at the University of Beirut, her mother had encouraged Karima to study advanced French and Arabic at the highly regarded Cross-Cultural Language Center in Paris. With her IQ well north of 130, she had excelled there, mastering the many Arabic dialects with her gifted ear and facile tongue. She could easily sort out the subtle differences between the Arabic spoken by the mountain tribes of Afghanistan and those of cities from Mogadishu in Somalia to Riyadh, Saudi Arabia.

Henri had secretly helped out with Karima's tuition. For her graduation, he had provided her with what they humorously now called 'The Paris Escape'. It was an extravagant gift indeed — the large, two-bedroom luxury flat in the lively Latin Quarter. Once settled there, she had found a well-paying job at the Eurocentres Language School, just a short walk away. Not surprisingly, Karima had flourished there too. Within three years she had become chairwoman of the highly regarded French Department.

"Should I be frightened?" she asked half-jokingly.

Henri squeezed her arm reassuringly. "I have no doubt America will greet you with open arms. Have no fear, my dear; your safety is my ultimate concern. I have made all the necessary arrangements."

Karima felt a shiver. Too much was happening, too quickly. She shook her head.

"No, no, *cher* Henri, this is going too fast," she said, gripping his hand tightly. "I am not sure who you are now. You sound like my Henri and yet somehow you are different."

Henri listened patiently.

"You are asking me to leave my life and go somewhere one ocean away, to a different culture, a different country. And that too at a time when my own country is in such turmoil and needs me the most."

"My dearest, trust me," said Henri earnestly. "You will do more for your country from America than in Beirut."

"I cannot go," said Karima, decisively. "This is too much." She looked directly at Henri and said, "I cannot leave my parents. A Muslim woman cannot just make this kind of decision and leave her family behind, even at my age."

"But what if they were to agree?" said Henri.

"They never would," said Karima firmly.

"Well let's go and ask them then," said Henri.

Meet The Parents

Henri gave directions to the fidgety taxi driver hunched over the steering wheel as if anticipating gunfire. He and Karima slid into the cab's back seat, which smelled of vintage perspiration and stale cigarettes.

The price of the ride was six times the daytime rate. Traveling anywhere near the war-torn Beirut Green Line during the daytime was always risky but after sunset the danger multiplied. The Green Line, so-called because trees and shrubs now occupied the vacant spaces of battle-scarred downtown Beirut, was now the epicenter of the conflict.

"You pay me now," the driver insisted, no doubt having been stiffed before.

Henri winced at the price but offered no argument, hearing a volley of distant gunfire, knowing that they were all putting their lives in potential danger. Fortunately, the driver knew several alternative routes and about twenty minutes later Karima and Henri were standing in front of a two-story brick building with a weather-worn sign over the front door which read 'PHARMACY'.

"Come back in two hours," Henri told the taxi driver.

"Same price."

Henry sighed. "Yes, same price."

The cobblestone alley alongside the pharmacy was dark but for a shaft of light from an upstairs window. Behind it stood a modest one-story home surrounded by a galvanized chain-link fence. Past an open gate was a door marked 'Do Not Enter'. Henri knocked.

Karima's mother Madalena opened it cautiously. She gave Karima a perfunctory hug and welcomed Henri formally into the foyer. Karima's father entered the room and greeted Henri with equal suspicion. They all knew Henri, of course, but he had never been to their home before. The uninvited, unannounced visit and at such a strange hour, they couldn't imagine.

After some cursory exchanges, Karima retreated with her parents to an adjoining room. Henri heard lowered voices, then the father's voice, louder than the others. Then all voices rose, a table was banged, and then things became subdued again. When they re-emerged, Karima's mother was dabbing at her eyes.

Karima's father addressed Henri directly.

"She cannot leave, she belongs here among our people. We have a pharmacy to run."

"The neighborhood and the pharmacy are dying, father," Karima argued. "And I'm dying with them."

Henri entered the conversation, speaking quietly and reasonably. "Perhaps I am to blame," he said. "This was my idea. I have been aware of Karima's linguistic brilliance for a while. I thought she would be wasting her talents here."

"Well, I have forbidden it." Hassam Salmady crossed his forearms, posturing his conviction, shaking his head dramatically.

"Let us leave," Madalena signaled to Karima, taking her elbow. "There is work to be done in the kitchen for feeding these two."

Once they were alone, Henri looked at the thin, angry man. "I believe you are on the same side as us, my friend. We are well aware."

Hassam's eyes lifted with curiosity. "We?" he said.

"Yes, we are well aware of your dedication to the cause."

Hassam spoke, in a lower tone now. "Go on."

Half an hour passed before the men emerged to eat. Hassam was looking more relaxed, almost smiling. Henri, taller, had an arm over his shoulder.

"Mr. Henri speaks with wisdom," he said. "He makes sense." He rubbed his hands. "And now, to dinner."

As Henri rose to return to his hotel, Karima was able to pull him aside and whisper to him in disbelief, "How did you convince him?"

Henri leaned in and whispered, "Let's just say that he saw the wisdom in your attending MIT to study cryptography and cryptanalysis."

"But isn't MIT in Boston? I thought you told me I was going to Washington."

"Shhh, my sweet," said Henri, getting into the waiting taxi. "Sometimes a man must be told what he wants to hear."

It had been absurdly easy to manipulate Hassam. By referring to 'we' rather than 'I', Henri had established that he was higher up some pecking order. Once he'd hinted that there was more money and a plan that hinged on his unique participation, Hassam had become considerably more pliant. He had readily agreed that a daughter in America at such a time would be safer than a daughter in Beirut.

"Back to the hotel?" the taxi driver asked.

"As fast as you can," said Henri.

Karima met him the next evening at his penthouse suite at the Hotel Albergo. It was Henri's suggestion that they dine there by his private swimming pool. Henri had ordered minced chicken kebabs over rice to be washed down with Pernod clouded with chilled rose water. Unlike their previous encounters at the Albergo, this one had a business-like air to it. There was work to be done.

Sitting at the wrought iron table by the swimming pool, Henri pulled out a large packet from his breast pocket. He went through the items one by one, handing each to Karima, who placed them in her purse.

"Your plane tickets."

"The address of your Washington, D.C., apartment."

"A key to your local post office box."

"Cash, a checkbook and a credit card from a D.C. bank."

"A letter of introduction to the Deputy Assistant of the United States State Department. And this."

Karima opened the passport just handed to her. It had her photo but next to it, what seemed like an error.

"Oh dear," she said. "I think they misspelled my name. It says Karissa. And, er, Smithson."

Henri laughed heartily. "Not a mistake, *ma cherie*. This is the new you. You will be reborn in the USA as Karissa Smithson. A small adjustment, I promise. As always, because your safety is paramount I felt that a more appropriate name would help ensure your success."

While Karima absorbed this, Henri continued.

"You were married six years ago to an Army First Lieutenant, George R. Smithson, who was assigned to the United Nations Assistance Mission during Rwanda's genocide of the Tutsis by the ruling Hutus. Your husband sadly went missing in action after his platoon was ambushed 30 miles northeast of Kigali in Rwanda's most mountainous region. Since then there has been no word of his whereabouts or condition. The current presumption is that he is dead. You as his wife have been made aware of this."

Stunned, the newly created Karissa Smithson exhaled anxiously and shook her head.

"A Foreign Service officer will meet you at the airport and take you to your apartment. I think you will like it, by the way." Henri winked.

With a slight wave of his skyward-pointing index finger, Henri closed the conversation. "One more thing. All those who now know you as Karima and wish to maintain contact must be told that communications should be sent to this post office address."

He handed Karima the final item in his packet.

Jackass

Karima Salmady looked down at her left hand. The simple gold band sparkled back at her, a mystery ever since Henri had slid it on her fourth finger just before their final embrace at the airport security gate. His last words to her were a strange mix of paternal and romantic sentimentality. Recalling them as she boarded the United Airlines direct flight to Washington, DC, she felt a rush of confusion and growing apprehension.

"My *petite* flower — or should I say my beautiful Karissa Smithson — please wear this ring. It will simplify your life. Perhaps some co-workers who want to court you will be discouraged by it. Your objectives will also be less encumbered."

What are my objectives? Karima wondered. *What had this relationship morphed into? And why exactly was she being sent to America? What exactly was she expected to be doing once she got there?*

Despite her inner doubts, Karima's transition to her Washington, D.C. job went quite smoothly, thanks for the most part to Henri's introductory documents and his attention to the minutest detail. The lavish apartment he had set up for her was perfect in every way, beautifully decorated and exactly to her taste. Where did the money for all this come from? How did Henri always manage to live so lavishly, far beyond the average diplomat's means? Years earlier, Karima had broached the subject.

"I make people disappear," was his answer.

After enjoying her astonishment for a moment, he laughed and revealed that he had worked briefly with France's Witness Protection Program. He seemed reluctant to elaborate and referred generally to the "tangled complexities of providing a person with a new identity".

"Tangled complexities?" Karima asked.

Henri answered carefully, "Sometimes people need to be relocated and reinvented so as not to be recognized by forces that might do them harm."

"And how exactly do you accomplish that?" Karima pressed.

"One needs help, of course — international realtors, document fabricators, discrete plastic surgeons, secret travel systems —" Henri trailed off. Making Karima 'disappear' to become Karissa was clearly not his first such project.

Karissa worked grueling 12-hour days. The rising threat of Islamic extremism made someone who spoke flawless Arabic and was familiar with the nuances of various dialects an invaluable national security asset. Many of her days were spent interpreting Muslim chatter for the Central Intelligence Agency and the National Security Agency. With her linguistic expertise, she moved rapidly up the ranks of various foreign affairs committees that required Arabic interpretations. She soon enjoyed a top-level security clearance that allowed her access to classified conversations.

Sundays gave her a much-needed respite from all this. Karima would typically don a running outfit, pull a baseball cap down to obscure her face and run eight miles before most of her neighbors had opened their eyes. Weather permitting, she would then cool down in one of the comfortable lounge chairs on her private outdoor balcony.

The only absolute work obligation on Sunday was the ritual of communicating with Henri, using the state-of-the-art communication system he had had installed just off the living room in Karissa's home office. An end-to-end encrypted call on the secure line was scheduled for noon Karissa's time, 7 pm Henri's time, and would usually last about an hour.

Henri was always intensely interested in things related to her work but especially anything pertaining to the broad sweep of Islamic activities. More recently, he had begun asking questions about the habits and perspectives of the current president.

"Well," said Karissa with some pride, "the President now requests my presence whenever CIA and NSA officials sit together for meetings."

Immediately Henri had questions. *Are the CIA and the NSA in competition? What do the intelligence agencies think of the president? Did you say the footprint of the West Wing has changed? Has the rear access to the White House changed as well?*

One day he asked, "So what's our Governor Lance Allworthy up to?"

"According to public opinion, in 1992 he will be a shoo-in for the White House," Karissa answered.

"No surprise there," said Henri. "Americans seem to be sick of their Congress and the current president's administration. They're thirsting for change and all the polls suggest that Lance Allworthy is the one who could deliver it."

Indeed, Lance was all over Virginia cutting ribbons and spending vast amounts of Virginia taxpayers' money on entitlements and political favors. His wagon of giveaway goodies even earned him the sobriquet of Governor Claus in certain quarters.

"He's planning a rally in Richmond next weekend," Karissa said.

"Shall we go?" Henri asked.

Karissa digested this for a moment before saying, "What? Aren't you in Europe?"

"Oh, didn't I mention it?" said Henri, laughing. "I'm coming to Washington the day after tomorrow."

Karissa suddenly felt the grip of Henri's control. She had been free all these months to dazzle her colleagues at work without a thought of Henri. Why didn't her heart leap this time at the thought of his coming to visit her?

A large and enthusiastic crowd had gathered at Capitol Square in the center of Richmond, Virginia, that cool-gray mid-June afternoon. Henri and Karissa had arrived early from D.C. to secure a position close to the podium behind which the presidential hopeful, the one and only Lance All-worthy, would speak. The media flooded the well-publicized event, scrambling for visual access. Banners, signs and flags were everywhere. Allworthy '92, Advance with Lance, 'Worthy For All.

Henri felt a wave of nausea as he and Karissa watched Lance perform, at his theatrical best, with the crowd roaring approval after each pronouncement.

Shaking his head, Henri turned to Karissa. "Do you really think this empty suit can deliver on his promises?"

Karissa shrugged, finding Henri's contempt vaguely unsettling. She was still finding her position in the jungle of American politics and was not quite sure where she stood regarding Lance.

Lance's speech ended with wild applause and he descended from the stage to mingle. The usual choreography followed, dazzling white smiles, energetic handshakes and, whenever the opportunity presented itself, a baby kissed.

"Your thoughts on the recent conflict in the Persian Gulf, Governor?" a reporter asked.

Lance hesitated, at a momentary loss for words.

"Ummm, it sure looks like the current administration is sending way too many troops in to protect Saudi Arabia."

"And you don't agree with this decision, Governor?"

Lance, suddenly pinned down and unable to deflect, stared at the reporter angrily for a moment. "Look, young fellow," he said, wagging a patronizing finger at him, "we've got all the oil we need, so I say let the Muslims figure out their problems on their own."

What a jackass, thought Henri.

The reporter wasn't letting go. "But Saudi Arabia has been one of our staunchest allies. It's the biggest country in the region, the second-largest producer of oil in the world and has the third biggest military and —"

"We don't need Saudi Arabia," Lance interrupted testily. "And the Middle East can go to hell for all I care."

Some jaws dropped.

Henri and Karissa returned to the apartment, their minds in different worlds. "Do you realize that one day you might be working for that clown?" Henri asked.

"You're right," said Karissa. "I hadn't thought of that."

The Joggers

Sunday morning euphoria usually came to Karissa when she hit the six-mile mark of her morning jog at a steady pace of five miles an hour. She was well-conditioned now and breezed easily past the narrow townhouses along her route through the affluent neighborhood of northwest Georgetown.

The air was crisper and the skies crystal clear now with winter just around the corner. There was even talk of light snow and perhaps a white Christmas. Not that that season held any particular meaning for her, but Karissa certainly enjoyed the growing festive spirit. Almost every door she passed was decorated with distinctive greens and bright red bows. Evergreens were new to this girl from Beirut. Her office, holiday festive in the past several weeks, had been humming an octave higher, with most of her coworkers sporting some form of Christmas attire. She herself had purchased a red sweater to complement her business slacks.

How strange but fascinating my world has become, she thought as her jog settled into its rhythm. The girl from a crowded quarter of Beirut is no longer Lebanese but now an American citizen, no longer Karima but Karissa. Henri's credentials had transformed her into a paradox. *Am I a spy?* Spending her days translating a clutter of Arabic and sharing her findings with a country that seemed not to like Muslims much certainly qualified as a spy-like pastime.

She could not deny that breathing the air of freedom was an invigorating experience for a girl with her cultural heritage. Indeed, life, liberty and the pursuit of happiness seemed like worthy values upon which to build a culture and a country.

But Karissa could not reconcile America's values with the adrenaline-soaked political chaos and civil unrest she saw around her. Friends had tried to explain the complex agendas and alignments behind the disorder but she was still far from understanding it. In the midst of all this, one person whose brilliance, clarity of thought and integrity had caught her attention was the Director of the CIA, Samuel Steele. At the confirmation hearing where she had most recently heard him speak, she had been impressed by his articulation of what internal and external security ought to mean in a successful democracy.

The key to sound democratic governance, Steele had said, was civilized discourse between parties and a willingness to compromise. Agencies like the CIA played a large role in creating the environment of security within which educated and inquiring citizens could feel free to exercise their constitutionally guaranteed rights. This included the right to give their informed consent to the policies proposed by the administration. Robust debate with the transparent and peaceful trade of ideas was the soul of a successful democracy and rested on the bedrock of a sense of security.

Karissa broke away from her political deliberations and looked both ways before crossing Wisconsin Avenue, heading towards the heart of historic Georgetown. She dropped the zipper of her top down by six inches to let some cool air in before resuming her jog.

And where did dear Henri fit into all of this? She sensed that there was a larger picture and that she was somehow a part of it. Henri had cleverly woven her into the fabric of his own plan, the exact nature of which was still a mystery to her. *Should I share my misgivings with someone? If so, who? Would I risk exposing myself if I took my concerns straight to the Director of the CIA?*

As it happened, the man on her mind was not all that far away. It had been Samuel Steele's long-standing ritual dating back to his college days to get in a good five-mile run every morning. Most days he liked the Anacostia Park river trail but recently, for a change of scenery, he'd explored an alternative route that took him down Wisconsin Avenue.

He had slid with customary confidence and only a few ripples into his new role as the Director of the CIA, a job that carried its share of intrigue, secrets and shadow operations. His compelling personality had bridged at least one important part of the new job: winning the respect and loyalty of the team with whom he would now be working. CIA staffers are notoriously loyal to their ex-bosses and getting their attention, much less their commitment, is no easy feat for a new appointee.

Steele was no stranger to taking calculated risks in exchange for an endorphin rush. The easy ones had been diving off the high cliffs of Acapulco and skiing down the icy mountain trails of Austria. More challenging was earning his colors and proving his mettle as a Special Operations SWAT team member for the FBI, and then climbing the ranks to become Director of the CIA.

Standing tall at 6 feet 3 inches and cinder-block solid, he cut quite a figure at public gatherings, his raw good looks undeniable. He had worn a shaved head for a decade, believing that a stylized haircut might suggest that he paid too much attention to his appearance. His smile revealed perfectly lined white teeth and his sharp-featured face was set with warm brown eyes. Having lost his young wife to the ravages of breast cancer had perhaps made him more sensitive than many others in his position.

He sometimes wondered if he would ever feel inclined to marry again; to re-experience such anguish from loss for a second time seemed unimaginable. Spending Christmas with his aging parents, who had loved his wife so much, was one of the most difficult events he forced himself to endure. Although recent years had presented him with feminine distractions aplenty he felt uninterested despite the emptiness in his heart.

As Steele broke into a burst of end-run speed, he noticed the figure of another jogger, a female in black workout leggings, about to cross the road up ahead. As he saw her profile, he recognized her.

Karissa leaned into the sharp right turn onto Grace Street from Wisconsin Avenue. There ahead was the cozy Dog Tag Bakery, a nonprofit operation run by disabled veterans, most famous for its warm fresh scones. Karima liked to end her run here, indulging herself with a freshly baked pastry.

Just about then, a voice somewhere behind her called out her name. She had still not gotten used to being called Karissa, and certainly 'Ms. Smithson' felt alien so her response was not immediate. By the time she turned to see who it was, the tall, handsome runner had reached her, steam rising from his shaved head.

"How nice to see you on this fine day, Ms. Smithson," said Samuel Steele, just slightly out of breath.

She now recognized the kind face in front of her. "Good morning to you too, er, Mr. Steele."

"Please call me Sam. After all, we're not yet on the clock," he said. His characterful face projected a warm sensitivity, unfamiliar to Karissa in a man. Even Henri, so unfailingly courteous, had not had such a quality.

Karissa smiled nervously, not quite sure what to say.

Sam rescued the moment. "I see you too enjoy this running thing."

"I do," Karissa said. "It gives me a chance to be evil and have a pastry now and then!" She nodded towards the bakery up ahead.

"Perhaps we can be evil together," Sam said, following her gaze.

They ordered coffee and a pair of strawberry scones. Karissa's eyes were riveted by the crumb hanging from Steele's lower lip.

Noticing her gaze, Steele laughed and swiped his mouth with a napkin, remarking, "You do know that your work has been absolutely indispensable, don't you? Especially with all the new chatter coming our way."

Karissa did not particularly want to talk shop, especially on a Sunday, but the company of this intriguing man gave her a sense of comfort and a curious openness to wherever he might wish to take the conversation.

The talk was easy and wandered through a variety of subjects. Steele shared the story of his wife and the details of her premature death. Karissa was tempted to mention a few benign bits of personal information but left it with just a vague reference to a mother who lived far away about whom she was worried. Anything more felt ill-advised.

As they rose to go their separate ways, Steele spoke with beguiling sincerity. "Ms. Smithson, we will no doubt see each other at work this week but I was wondering — would you consider joining me for a run next Sunday?"

For a few moments, Karissa was completely caught off guard. Was this really happening? Did she need this? She hardly knew anything about Steele except that he was way out of her league. Her sense of humor took over.

"Only if we stop at the bakery," she said, managing to keep a straight face.

Steele smiled and offered a handshake.

"Deal!"

Free For All

The slogan on the side of the chartered luxury campaign bus, All for Worthy, left little doubt as to who was inside as the mobile executive office zigzagged across America's heartland before arriving in Des Moines, the capital of Iowa. It was here in early August that Lance Allworthy and his entourage began their full-court press on the American voter at the Iowa State Fair — a political free-for-all where even the most delusional outlier could soapbox his or her presidential aspirations at an audience of over 100,000 daily attendees.

Lance recalled with satisfaction his gripping evangelical stump speech and the taste of the bacon-wrapped corn-battered hot dog on a stick that was Iowa's signature culinary offering as the country's largest producer of pork.

Except perhaps Virginia's state legislature and the US congress, he thought to himself with a smirk.

Augusta's attempt at eating the gourmet corn dog had triggered one of her nastier migraines.

As the bus now headed back to Virginia, Augusta massaged her right hand as she recalled the endless rolling hills and cornfields of Iowa. "If I'd shaken the hand of one more hog farmer I think my fingers would have fallen off."

Five months later, in early February, the bus was back in Iowa to honor the quirky tradition of the Iowa caucuses, the first real contest in the presidential nomination process. A rapacious media saw Lance as the uncontested Democratic candidate as he captured the overwhelming majority of delegates who had responded to his rhapsodic rhetoric and the brilliant, switch-on smiles that he and Augusta had by now perfected into a fine art.

"The power couple of the century," read The National Enquirer in every grocery store checkout line across the country. "A genius pair at self-promotion." The political circus had begun in earnest and Lance and Augusta had found the big top, the main tent, and flooded the swooning public with waves of patriotic optimism.

The New Hampshire presidential primary followed on the historically designated fourth Tuesday in February, and was considered a bellwether for how the candidate would fare in a general election. As Lance was unopposed, the massive media coverage of the traditional debate at Dartmouth College morphed into a campaign rally.

"It is time your government took better care of you." Lance said, eyes piercing the audience. When the foot-stomping and applause died down, Lance leaned into the microphone and said in a conspiratorial whisper, "And I'm the man to make that happen."

A young reporter raised his hand and stood up without being recognized and posed a question. "Sir, wouldn't your ideology create a dependent population controlled by an overreaching government? A monarchy? An autocracy? Or perhaps even the risk of a dictatorship?"

Lance smiled appreciatively, as though this was the very question he had been waiting for. He knew his answer would be lost in the general cacophony. "That's a perfect question, young man," he said. "And you're 100% correct. Your government does indeed know what's best for you."

The wave of redlined public adoration carried Lance right up to a landslide Super Tuesday which secured his nomination at the Democratic National Convention in New York's Madison Square Garden.

Crowned as the country's democratic savior from the current Republican administration, his actual run for president was equally lopsided. Rumors from reliable, albeit unknown sources, put the Republicans at a distinct disadvantage, with a seemingly biased media machine recklessly eviscerating the Republican candidate, spewing questions of tax evasion, infidelity and corruption.

The presidential debate sealed the deal. The war of words was a massacre, with Lance's silver tongue pistol-whipping his crumbling opponent. It was political theater at its finest.

Augusta sat in the front row watching the performance until the moderator closed the debate and Lance moved toward his vanquished opponent, hand extended. The shattered Republican turned away in surrender. Augusta was the first on stage with a spousal congratulatory hug.

"Well done, my Cicero," she whispered. "Well done."

Only two weeks remained before election day. Lance radiated the confidence of a Goliath.

"The White House will be our castle," he whispered back. "I'll be king and you, I presume, will be my gorgeous queen."

Augusta smiled as they waved to the adoring audience.

Henri could not take his eyes off the televised debate. Every network covered it. The image in his mind was of America's golden boy in a very different place and time, standing half-naked with his pants around his ankles in a Paris alley, gushing uncontrollably all over a woman of the night.

A New President

Through a blizzard of red, white and blue confetti and the raucous cheers of the crowd, the expression on Lance Allworthy's face could best be called a gloat. By his side, Augusta was waving, throwing kisses and thumbs-ups to the audience. Lance worked the stage with high-fives and skyward fist pumps. He pointed his finger at different spots in the room and broadened his smile.

"Who is he pointing to?"

Karissa was sitting barefoot next to Samuel Steele twiddling her toes. Their eyes were glued to the television.

"Nobody he knows," said Steele. "It's an old political trick. Point and grin. As if everyone in the audience is your friend. It's a political lovefest."

The swing states of Michigan, Pennsylvania and Florida had all gone Democrat and swung early. Thankfully, the victory celebration did not have to wait until the wee hours of the morning.

Sam Steele slapped his thigh, "He's got it!"

"He's won?" Karissa, still confused by the electoral college process, tilted her head in question. "Is it over then, America's love affair with candidate Lance Allworthy?"

"Some might say the love affair has just begun," said Steele with a chuckle. "He's got over 270 electoral college votes now and that makes him the winner. The White House is his. He's going to be our new boss."

Karissa wasn't sure what this meant for her.

"I don't think your job will change much but the President may choose a new head for his CIA," said Steele.

"Why?"

"One reason could be that I'm a Republican."

"So?" Karissa frowned.

"Allworthy is a Democrat so he and I may not see eye to eye on some issues. Of course, the position of CIA Director is non-political and my Republican affiliation ought not to be a factor but these are partisan times. Allworthy has not exposed his true colors yet. Politicians running for office are masters at the art of deflection and dissembling, delivering evasive answers and shifting blame. It can be hard to know what they really stand for until after they've won, and even then you don't necessarily know for sure."

"Should we join the downtown celebrations?" asked Karissa. "I can already hear firecrackers and shouting."

The two briskly walked the eighteen blocks to O street. Crowds milled about the waterfront Cambria Hotel and Convention Center where the President-elect was to deliver his victory speech. A teletron flashed an image of his soon-to-be chief of staff, Sophia Slack, who would introduce him. Behind her stood the waving President-elect and the next First Lady, as well as Vice President-elect Maxwell Donahue with his wife. The cheers inside and outside the Convention Center were deafening.

After about half an hour, Karissa and Steele retreated to a bar three blocks away and ordered two Cokes and a bowl of ice cream with two spoons.

"There will be some changes," Sam said, licking the chocolate off the back of his spoon.

"Meaning?"

"Democrats think big government is the answer. They feel they know what's best for everyone and like to impose their regulatory policies on American citizens whether they like them or not. They like controlling things, your education, your job, your healthcare, the economy, immigration, anything they can get their hands on. And they'll tax the hell out of you to do it."

"And the Republicans?" Karissa asked, her tongue catching the last drop of ice cream off her spoon.

"Different story. They're more about individual freedom,

less regulation and smaller government." Steele paused to wipe his mouth with his napkin. "And more pride in America and her history."

How complicated, Karissa thought. Recalling her recent phone conversation with Henri, she found herself questioning his feelings toward America. What was his personal ideology? If he were American, would he have been a Democrat or a Republican? She had no idea. His plans, whatever they were, seemed independent of the party in power. It was his specific opinion of Lance that baffled her.

Around 10 pm, Steele accompanied Karissa back to her apartment and then jogged back to his own.

"President-elect Allworthy and soon-to-be First Lady, it is my great pleasure."

Frieda Krause, the cool, 60-year-old director of the White House Transition Team, dipped her head respectfully toward Lance. She had been an up-close witness to the idiosyncrasies of four previous presidents and their families and staff, and knew well that most of them came with at least one load of dirty laundry. The epitome of Prussian discipline, her silver gray hair was tightly bound into a perfect bun, and you wouldn't see a single wrinkle on her tailored White House uniform. It fell to her to give the incoming President his first detailed tour of the White House that would be his center of operations for the next four years. For Lance Allworthy, who could not stop smiling smugly, it was a defining moment. Augusta, now wife of the world's most powerful man, also seemed to openly relish it.

"Step this way please."

They toured the White House in a leisurely fashion, accompanied by several other transition team members.

"There are six levels to the White House, with 25 bathrooms and 28 fireplaces. . ." Augusta wondered how anyone could possibly decorate that many fireplaces by Christmas.

The tour ended in the West Wing, which contained the Oval Office, the Cabinet Room and the Situation Room, and the Roosevelt Room in the basement below.

"It is customary for the incoming President to redecorate the Oval Office to suit his personal tastes."

The outgoing President and First Lady had had the walls painted a soft yellow and hung artwork from several museums as well as the White House collection of historic paintings. The large ceiling medallion of an eagle had been there for four decades as had the long-case Federal "grand-daddy" clock. The fern-green carpet contained a central presidential seal and the two high-back chairs flanking the fireplace, where heads of state shook hands with the President, were upholstered in gold brocade.

Then there was Lance's official workplace. The iconic 1,300-pound hand-carved Resolute Desk, Ms. Krause disclosed, was made with timber from the British frigate HMS Resolute which had been frozen in the Arctic ice and rescued by the American Navy in 1854.

Portraits of George Washington, Andrew Jackson and Norman Rockwell graced the west wall. A bronze by Frederic Remington sat on a pedestal next to the north door.

The White House head of interior design and the White House curator next looked at Augusta.

"Shall we?"

The three exited through the east door of the Oval Office into the Rose Garden.

"The redecoration budget is a maximum of 1.75 million dollars," said the interior designer. "It's yours to deploy as you wish. Traditionally, the First Lady also gives thought to how she would like the White House gardens to look. Our staff is here to help you any way we can."

Augusta smiled, taking pleasure in the authority she now wielded to make the White House her own.

"This way, please," Frieda Krause said to Lance, pointing towards a door. "I'm sure Madam First Lady would want to explore the estate."

Within the Cabinet Room, Sophia Slack, Lance's choice for Chief of Staff, was sitting at the end of the large mahogany table, surrounded by comfortable Corinthian leather armchairs, each with a blank brass plates across the back that soon would be engraved with the names of the members of the President's new cabinet. The walls were gray, the rug a robin's eggshell blue.

Standing to greet Lance, Slack invited him to take the

chair next to hers. Her smile turned business-like as she presented him with a large thick notebook with the words PRESIDENT'S COPY across the cover.

"This is a compilation of current domestic and international issues with which you might want to become familiar, along with some talking points," she said. "In the upcoming weeks, more formal and detailed briefings from agency heads are scheduled on these subjects."

Lance looked down at the four-inch-thick notebook with tabs along the side indicating the subject of each entry: Los Angeles Racial Riots/Police Brutality, NAFTA/Mexico Canada agreement, Hurricane Andrew/Florida Damage, Minnesota's Largest Mall in the World Opens, Iraq Hampers UN Weapons Inspectors, Supreme Court Okays Abortion Rights.

Lance scratched his head and looked at Slack. "A lot going on here," he said, hiding his inner trepidation. He flipped to a new topic in the notebook: Earth Summit/Climate Change. And then the next. And the next.

"I have a question, Sophia," Lance said. "What is this thing called the worldwide web that everyone's talking about?" he asked.

Understanding new technology had never been one of Lance's strong suits.

"I'd be happy to set up a special presentation at your convenience to update you on this emerging technology, Mr President-elect," said Slack.

It all seemed like too much work to Lance. There was so much to learn but did he really need to learn it all? Wasn't it more important to hire people who knew what needed to be known and did what had to be done so that he didn't have to bother?

Lance and Augusta were eventually reunited in the backseat of a black Cadillac Escalade driven by a newly appointed member of the Secret Service. Lance turned to Augusta.

"So, Madam First Lady?"

Augusta smiled. "It's beyond anything I've dreamed of, darling," she said.

"I'm glad," said Lance. "You can see you married exactly the right man."

"Didn't I just?" Augusta snuggled against him. "But —"

"But what?" asked Lance.

"But do you think you're up to the job?"

Am I in too deep? Can I do this? For a few moments, Lance felt a wave of panic though his face betrayed nothing. Then Augusta saved the moment for him, answering her own question.

"Of course, you are, Lance Allworthy. You're Superman."

Cleo's Secret

President-elect Lance and Augusta invited their families for a holiday dinner at the beautifully decorated Governor's Mansion in Richmond, Virginia. Kat and ET saw this as a synthetic gesture by Lance to assuage his own guilt for being such a non-member of the family he had so ruthlessly exploited since his boyhood.

"I know, darling," said ET. "I'm afraid it's going to be a bit awkward."

"For you and Cleo more than for me," Kat said. "Lance never really connected with me at any level." She knew about the supposedly secret allergy jabs Cleo gave Lance. And then there was ET's history as 'official' photographer to Lance.

"Anyway, Officer Haynes," Kat said, rubbing her hands briskly. "This year, I've found the perfect gift for the family."

ET raised a puzzled eyebrow. "For everyone?"

"Yup. This gift is going to get everybody's attention. And I mean everybody!"

"Well, well, Mrs. Claus, you sure have dialed me up to ten with curiosity."

ET felt strangely embarrassed as he turned the faded blue Ford Taurus onto East Broad Street. The historic gates into Capitol Square and the governor's house lay ahead. ET reached into his pocket and pulled out the formal dinner invitation and presented it to the security guard. Once under the Doric columns of the portico, ET brought the car to a stop and engaged the emergency brake, reaching behind for his camera bag. While one white-gloved marine helped Kat out, another opened the driver's side door and smartly saluted ET as he stepped out.

With her clutch purse in one hand and a large shopping bag in the other, Kat swiveled toward her husband to ask, "Ready for this?"

ET grinned, "Let the games begin!"

They entered the pale yellow, federal-style residence. Built in 1813, the structure was lush with history and furnished with the finest of American antiques. Lance had once boasted that dignitaries such as Teddy Roosevelt and Winston Churchill had stayed there, implying none too subtly that he was somehow their peer.

Upstairs, as they entered a short hallway and approached Lance and Augusta's private living quarters, Kat adjusted her tidy, contoured outfit. Her dress, with bright splashes of green and red, had Christmas written all over it. ET playfully pulled a Santa cap out of his pocket and said, "Do you know what I really want for Christmas?"

"That this evening doesn't run on too long?"

"Well, that too!"

The door burst open and the soon-to-be First Lady of the United States swept out into the hall wearing a bright red dress and a pair of flats with bells attached to the tassels. A flurry of customary hugs was exchanged.

"So where's the mistletoe?" ET joked as the three moved inside. Across the room, Cleo raised her wine glass in the direction of the new arrivals.

"Ho, ho, ho!" she called out, with uncharacteristic humor, a rare smile lighting up her face.

A more formal "Happy holidays!" was heard from the other side of the room as Lance strode out, glass in hand.

"And a Merry Christmas to you too, Mr. President-elect!" Kat said. "Less than a month until the inauguration!"

Octavia and Horace Carnegie rose simultaneously from two side chairs and waved. As expected, their greetings to ET and Kat combined condescension with pomposity.

Lance cut into the awkward silence. "Did you bring your camera, ET? I think a shot of Augusta and me by the tree she helped decorate would be a nice treat for the press before we move out of this place."

"Can you remember the last time I was near you and didn't have at least a handy point-and-shoot camera with me?" ET responded.

The photo session ended quickly and another round of drinks was served. As Lance handed Kat and ET each a fresh glass, Cleo thought she detected just the slightest tremor in her brother's hand. The medical side of her was trying to make sense of it. Could it be nerves? Stress? Something even more worrisome?

Dinner came promptly at eight. The ceremonial cutting of the prime rib roast fell, as per tradition, to Lance. The hungry family members watched as he sharpened his knife with the theatrics of a military drummer boy. But midway through the production, while cutting a generous slice of the beef, Lance seemed to lose his grip on the carving knife, letting it fall to the floor with a clatter.

"Goddamn it!" he shouted as he bent down and clumsily retrieved the knife, its edge dripping pink juices from the roast onto the cream-colored carpet.

Augusta jumped in. "Let me take that knife to the kitchen, dear, and rinse it off."

Thus did dinner unfold, full of random chatter, forced small talk and uneasy silences. Half an hour later, pushing back from his chair, ET held his belly, "That was truly delicious, right down to the cranberry cheesecake!"

"Hear, hear!" Kat concurred, toasting the host and hostess. Lance offered brandy in response to her suggestion that they gather around the tree and open their gifts.

"Here's the drill," Kat said. "Everyone has to open their gift from me at the same time."

Ribbons were snipped and discarded, followed by the sounds of paper being ripped. Lance was the first to read the label identifying the gift. "A DNA kit! Well, I'll be damned."

ET, looking pointedly at Kat, said with a glint, "I guess this will confirm that I am a direct descendant of Casanova."

Kat rolled her eyes, smiling affectionately at him, and said, "Now that's one thing I do not need proof of, mister." Then, turning to the others, she said brightly, "Well? Do you like it? It's the latest technology, I thought it would be so interesting to know more about our ancestry!"

Augusta, holding her box, looked up at Lance, who seemed perplexed. "Yes, of course," he said, hesitantly.

"Of course," Augusta repeated mechanically.

Octavia turned to Horace. "There will be no surprises for us, my dear. You'll find that we carry aristocratic British blue blood all the way back to the crusades. Right, honey?"

Cleo looked into her glass of wine. Her thoughts slightly dulled by the food and drink, she struggled to grasp the implications of Kat's unusual gift. And then it hit her. What would Lance's results reveal? A lump formed in her throat. Her mind went dancing down the years to the dreadful secret she had stumbled upon when they had all been children. She still vividly remembered the events of that evening.

She had been ten. As was typical back then, her parents were attending some kind of sporting event that showcased Lance, who was already showing signs of being an exceptional athlete. Katherine and Cleo were spending the weekend with their grandparents, something they both enjoyed. Cleo especially felt a warmth and acceptance from Grampa and Nana that she'd never experienced at home.

There had been an especially lively discussion over dinner about various family activities past and present. Grampa and Nana were particularly proud that their son Carl Allworthy — Cleo's and Kat's father — had invented a breathable hot-weather fabric ideal for sportswear. It launched him and led to the creation of his own line of fashionable, high-end athletic apparel. The only downside to his remarkable success was the constant travel, a lot of it to China where he had a manufacturing base.

That evening, unable to sleep, young Cleo thought a cookie and some milk might help. At the top of the staircase, she overheard her grandparents still talking downstairs, voices raised with obvious emotion. *If only I had turned around and gone back to bed.*

"It's obvious he's not our grandson," Grampa was saying. "His looks and mannerisms don't resemble Carl's at all. There is no way Lance is our flesh and blood."

Cleo gasped in disbelief as more details emerged.

About nine months before Lance was born, Carl had been in China for several weeks on business. The grandparents had offered to babysit Cleo and Katherine so that their mother could attend her weekly church choir practice. Grampa had gone out to pick something up for supper and driven by Carl's house on the way back. He'd noticed that the lights were off in the main house but several dim lights were on in the adjacent guest house. A dark car stood parked behind some bushes.

When the grandparents babysat the following week, there it was again, the same car in the same shadows, the same dim lights in the guest house. While Grampa watched from his parked car, a tall muscular man emerged from the front door. His tight, slicked-back golden curls glistened in the bright slant of light from the street lamp. He looked up, then left and right. His eyes were electric blue.

The man quickly entered the car parked in the shadows and eased out onto the street before turning the headlights on. As the dark sedan sped off Grampa noticed the rear license plate, with a sense of recognition. There were plenty of black sedans with tinted windows in town but only one had a license plate that read VOTE4ME.

Moments later, there was another shock just as he was about to turn on the ignition. The guest house's door opened again and a woman emerged discreetly, tidying her hair. It took but a moment for Grampa to recognize his daughter-in-law. So much for "choir practice".

From that evening, Cleo's relationship with Lance changed forever. She could never look at him without remembering Grampa's voice: "There is no way he is our flesh and blood."

Her parents and grandparents were now long gone and Cleo was the only one in the family who knew this dark secret. Her brother, President-elect of the United States, had no clue that he had an amoral politician for a father and an adulteress for a mother.

If he only knew.

Where's Henri?

Karissa turned the key to open the post office box, not expecting to find anything inside. Her heart bumped as she recognized her mother's handwriting on a small collection of letters waiting there. Several lengthy letters Karissa had written to her mother so far had gone unanswered and she had become increasingly worried that something might be terribly wrong back home. That the name Karima Salmady appeared on the letters was another jolt, reminding her of the simpler life she had lived before becoming Karissa Smithson. The thought crossed her mind that Henri must also have a key to her mailbox. Had he already steamed open these letters and read them?

Karissa dashed to her apartment and dropped into the chair nearest the window before opening the first letter.

Beirut, May 6, 1993

My dearest Mima,

Thank you for your letters. They were discovered in a pile of your father's papers. I don't know how many others you have written that might have escaped me.

I so wish you were here but I am also so happy to hear that life in America agrees with you. I am so proud of your success working for the government!

But oh! How I miss my Mima!

The weather here has been hot and difficult, adding to the sad state of affairs. There is danger everywhere as several Muslim and Christian factions seem committed to destroying our city, not to mention each other. 'Death to the Infidels!' graffiti is everywhere. Some posters call America the 'Great Satan of the World'.

It is also with a heavy heart that I tell you that all is not well with your father. I can no longer make sense of him. He has slipped into a most sinister and suspicious disposition. There is no conversation between us any more; it is as though I no longer exist for him. Sometimes, he disappears for several weeks at a time. Indeed, the pharmacy has been closed more than it has been open in the last two months. How we survive financially is a mystery and a miracle.

I hope I can get this letter to the post
without your father knowing. His anger at
my writing such things would be beyond
measure. I can't begin to imagine.

Please write to me. I will pray
your reply reaches me safely.

Your loving Mumum

PS: I will continue to use the post office address
you gave me until you inform me otherwise.

Karissa gazed out the window without seeing, her mind numb and knotted up. She was deeply rattled by her mother's letter. Guilt welled up within her that she wasn't there to comfort the woman who had single-handedly raised her and encouraged and supported her academic development.

Karissa slid her index finger under the envelope flap and opened another letter.

Beirut, August 9, 1993

My dearest Mima,

I cannot be sure that my letters will find you but
I must continue to write. You are my lifeline now.
Two weeks ago, your father left home with no
explanation as to where he was going or when
he would return. He gave me $10,000 dollars in

cash in a large envelope the day before he left.

*I am even more frightened after some of the things
I witnessed at the pharmacy while he was here.
A man entered one day — a rare event to have
an actual paying customer these days — and
requested an antibiotic that I could not locate.
This is what made me enter the back room where
your father was, to ask him if he knew where
I could find the medicine. Your father was in
a meeting with several men, three younger-
looking and one more elderly. Their conversation
sounded hushed and urgent. Large amounts of
cash were on the table and a good many electronic
devices, including some new mobile phones,
were being placed in a shipping container.*

*When your father noticed me, he turned toward
me as if to hide what was happening behind
him. He looked annoyed by my intrusion
and ordered me to go back to the store.*

*Oh, Mima! I have been so nervous since that
day. I worry and remain frightened at what
tomorrow will bring. Beirut has become even
more of a scary place. The city market, which used
to be filled with people and friendly conversation,
is now almost deserted. People whisper in low
tones. There is suspicion and caution everywhere.*

*I miss you, my dear — so very much. I am glad
you have found America to your liking but
I wish so much that we could be together.*

*Please write. For now, mail still seems
to come to the pharmacy address.*

Your loving Mumum

Karissa's hand, with the letter, dropped to her lap. A part of her was deeply shaken and troubled by all that she had read. She longed to be with her mother, to hold and comfort her in her loneliness and fear in that war-torn city. But another part of her, the quick-thinking, razor-sharp analyst, had noticed an anomaly: it was not just her father who had gone missing.

Was it a coincidence? It had been months since she'd been with Henri. The old Henri she had loved was no longer in evidence. During the last three weeks, even the usual Sunday phone calls had stopped.

The crazy thought crossed her mind that perhaps her father and Henri somehow knew each other better than they had let on. Perhaps they were even working together. But no sooner did this idea cross her mind than she dismissed it. It was too absurd to be true.

But it left a gaping question in her mind: *Where's Henri?*

Steele Has An Idea

There had been no sleep for Karissa. Her mind had thrashed about wildly all night long, roiling with thoughts about all that was going on, still grappling with the implications of her mother's letters and Henri's disappearance. She rose from her bed at first light, stretched and put on her Sunday jogging outfit, preparing for her 9 a.m. ritual with Samuel Steele.

As she turned on the coffee maker, she looked down at the note that had come from Henri the day before.

> *My Sweet Karissa,*
>
> *It is time I come and visit you. Thirty days more, and I promise you will see me again. I miss mon petit chou so much.*
>
> *Henri*

Indeed, after the long days of silence, the note and its faux romantic sentiments sounded hollow. The thought of meeting Henri again did not, for the first time, quicken her pulse. So many things had changed. So many questions. She looked down at her cup of coffee and said aloud, "Who am I to him now?" Their romantic, erotic past life together, filled with glorious memories, was in ruins. Now she was simply his informant, perhaps even his spy.

The epiphany came as she sat nursing her coffee: *It's all about Henri!* He was at the heart of everything that was troubling her. For a moment a strange sense of loss came over her before being replaced by a wave of calm resolve.

She laced her running shoes. She knew what to do. Today the wall would come down, whatever the consequences.

Nursing their bottled water after their run, Sam Steele and Karissa were sitting face to face, having just finished their pastry at the Dog Tag Cafe. Steele had listened intently without judgment or interruption as Karissa slowly, carefully disclosed details of her life before coming to America. Leaving out only the bit about her conversion from Karima Salmady to Karissa Smithson, she told Steele about the dominant role Henri had played in so many aspects of her early life, her education and her maturing into a woman. She spoke of how over the years he had become "more serious, more sinister, more opaque".

While Sam outranked her as a civil servant, she somehow felt his equal in human terms. His manner was respectful and obviously concerned. As their conversation progressed, Karissa relaxed, feeling more comfortable.

"Does Mr. Duchamp frighten you?" Steele asked.

Karissa thought for a moment before answering, "No, he does not scare me. But he does not fool me either. He tries to make me think everything between us is as it's always been. But he has changed and I can see it."

"He worries me," Sam said. "He sounds devious, judging by his transformation from a supposed romantic to someone so dark and covert."

"He has always described himself as a cultural attaché," Karissa added.

"Whatever that is," Sam said.

"He wrote to me a few days ago, after a long silence. He wants to see me, here in D.C."

"Is he coming then?" asked Sam.

"In thirty days, according to his note to me."

The CIA Director's antennae were now fully extended, "Perhaps we have an opportunity here. We must find out more about this Mr. Duchamp."

Tears suddenly welled up in Karissa's eyes, embarrassing her that she could not hide her confusion and anxiety from this man. Steele offered her a napkin and waited.

"Things are different now," she said. "We were lovers once. We enjoyed each other, there was humor, joy — innocent exuberance."

"But now things are not the same," Sam noted, a question spoken like a statement.

"I first caught a glimpse of a different side of him some years ago while we were on holiday in Cyprus for a few days. We visited the grave site of his parents. That was when I realized that only his father was Christian. His mother was Muslim, though they had been buried side by side in a Christian graveyard."

Sam nodded, eyebrows arching in curiosity.

"He was preoccupied that entire trip," Karissa continued. "Something was on his mind. The war in Lebanon was going on, Christians against Muslims. I think something changed in him that day. He seemed to embrace Islam after that with a zeal that felt like he was making up for lost time."

"I see," Sam said.

Karissa took a sip of water. "Now he grills me for information about all the Arabic babble I am asked to translate. He doesn't like President-elect Allworthy, that's for sure."

Have I said too much? Karissa wondered. *Why is Steele looking so serious? Should I have shared this information sooner? Am I in trouble now?*

Sam sensed her discomfort but pressed on. "And Mr. Duchamp's upcoming visit? What do you expect?" he asked.

Karissa thought for a moment. "He'll try to make me feel that nothing has changed between us."

"Just like old times."

Aware of venturing into intimate territory, Sam spoke delicately. "Would that include — romance as well?"

"I don't understand," said Karissa.

"Will there be sex?" Steele asked bluntly. "And my apologies if that sounded intrusive, Karissa."

Karissa blushed. "It has been a part of our, well, relationship," she said. "He'll expect it."

To Karissa, sharing these long-held secrets was a relief, like a load lifting off her shoulders. Somehow the conversation made her and Sam more than running partners, more like collaborators. It was as though they were now on a mission together.

"Are we going to expose Henri Duchamp?" she asked.

Steele leaned forward, their faces conspiratorially close now. "Do you know what GPS stands for?" he asked.

Perfect Timing

Karissa matched Henri's thrusting with her own. She had to make him believe it was real. Like old times. Almost. She knew from past experience that Henri's climax could sometimes come without warning, which meant that she might have just minutes to complete her task. To make things more challenging, her only practice had been with a rubber human dummy.

She thought her performance of faux passion so far had been credible. She had bitten him on his arms and neck, taking him by surprise. He yelped with the sharp pain but underplayed it, saying, "Oh my, someone has missed her Henri very much."

Her CIA instructors had been explicit. Bite him in three or four places so that the main one will be one of many.

She could sense the quickening of his movements. The end wouldn't be far now. As though on cue, Henri drew a sharp breath and arched as he emptied himself rhythmically and deeply into Karissa's thrusting loins. At the peak of his pleasure, Karissa wrapped her arms around him and moaned, digging her fingernail deep into the soft tissue between Henri's shoulder blades. Henri cried out and stiffened as the sudden pain mingled with the consuming pleasure of his own climax.

Moments later, they lay in a heaving mound of tangled limbs, the sweat glistening on their bodies. After several minutes, they withdrew from each other.

"You wounded me," Henri said, half serious, half joking. "Would you take a look at the damage, *cherie?*"

"But of course," she said, leading him into the bathroom. She inspected the wound she had caused, dabbing the blood away with a cotton ball. It was a perfect job: she could see the glinting edge of the small micro-device that she had embedded under his skin.

"You're bleeding, *cheri*," Karissa said. "I am so sorry, I didn't realize how much I had missed you. Will you ever forgive me?"

"A woman's passion, even when it is painful, is always a badge of pride for a man, my sweet," said Henri.

"What can I say — you bring out the tigress in me. I promise I shall cut my claws shorter the next time. Now let me apply some healing salve and a bandage."

Later, they ate in silence, a Caesar salad with blackened salmon. Without words, they returned to the bedroom and fell into a deep sleep, turned away from each other.

Henri was the first to leave the bed the next morning, heading straight into the bathroom. While he showered, Karissa reviewed the events of the previous day. He had arrived early Sunday afternoon, carrying a bouquet of mixed spring flowers and a bottle of their favorite French champagne.

Their obligatory hug had been too tight to be heartfelt but while in the clinch, Karissa had smelled a faintly familiar but elusive organic odor emanating from his clothes.

After lunch, the expected interrogation began, focused and unapologetically aggressive.

What can you tell me of the President's current routine?

What do you know of the CIA Director?

What is the current status of US intelligence on domestic terrorist locations?

At one point, Henri had said, somewhat cryptically, "Your role in all of this is critical, my dear Karissa."

But Karissa was not taken in so easily this time. With brilliant agility, she disclosed very little new or meaningful information that Sunday afternoon.

Interrupting her thoughts, Henri appeared at the doorway of the bedroom, showered and dressed.

"I must be off now," he announced, as if in a hurry. Karima almost asked him where he was going but stopped herself, realizing that his whereabouts would be a matter of permanent record now that she had planted the GPS chip in his back.

Walking up to Karissa, who was still lazing on the bed, Henri leaned down and placed a kiss on her cheek. "It has been my pleasure, my dear, dear Karissa," he whispered. "You will never be forgotten."

With that, he was gone, leaving Karissa with a single thought — *Why had that felt so much like a last goodbye?*

In Absentia

The first 22 months of Lance Allworthy's presidency had consisted of reiterated promises that his public still seemed to feel he would keep, as well as a whirlwind of new and noble intentions. Despite the lack of any significant achievements, Lance had enjoyed a surprisingly lengthy political honeymoon. His adoring voters did not seem to care about his inclination to indulge himself in the grandeur of his position, thinking naively that he was busy behind the scenes addressing the needs of a nation in desperate need of repair. The media, for the most part, refused to be critical, promoting instead the narrative that the president was indeed working hard on behalf of the American people, signing a series of executive orders in an attempt to undo all "the damage done to the United States by the previous administration".

The majority of Lance's appointees were sycophants mostly interested in furthering their own personal and political interests. His yes-men were perfectly happy to ride the coat-tails of their commander-in-chief for as long as he was able to ride the wave of popular public opinion.

The moral elasticity of Lance's White House permitted certain activities of questionable propriety. Most noteworthy of these was doubtless the Allworthy Foundation, which Lance set up during his first year in office.

"The mission of the foundation will be to address the issue of world hunger and raise funds for the cause through a vast network of philanthropic international partners with deep pockets," he told Augusta.

While appearing to be a strictly humanitarian organization with nothing but charitable intentions, the Foundation also put Lance in touch with important world leaders and influential officials willing to open up their coffers and provide a steady stream of contributions.

"And you, Mr. President, will doubtless find numerous ways to show your gratitude to these various patrons," said Augusta, with a knowing smile.

"Precisely," said the President, with a straight face.

Lance handpicked from his most loyal and subservient minions to make up the Foundation's first board of directors, including First Lady Allworthy as an honorary member.

Arguably the most pliable member of this team was

former gridiron teammate Vice President Maxwell Donahue, who had agreed to monitor the foundation's accounts and sign the checks.

An accountant after leaving the army, Donahue had been a highly visible auditor for one of the largest Democrat Political Action Committees until Lance had tapped him as a running mate, sensing that his meek personality would also make him a perfect scapegoat, should that need ever arise.

If there was a wake-up moment for Lance, it was the midterm elections. It would be an understatement to say that he was shaken by the results. A segment of the voting public had finally started to pay attention. Gallup and Rasmussen polls showed the Democrat's approval rating plummeting well below 50 percent. The party took a thrashing, with both the House and the Senate going red. Middle America had spoken.

The only one who seemed completely unsurprised by the outcome was Augusta. "Americans outside Washington's beltway bubble and east of whacko California and a few left-wing cities are not stupid," she said coolly.

"What are you trying to say?" asked Lance.

"A neutral observer looking at your presidency would see a country in a mess and a public impatient for solutions — and a President who is for all intents and purposes AWOL."

Lance arched his eyebrows in surprise.

"Oh, I know, baby, you've been working so hard and you have so much you want to do but — the neutral observer does not see it that way. Neutral observers suck. So they say things like the buck stops with you, Mr. President, even though you and I know it stops with the houses of Congress. And they feel their Superman needs to do better even though Superman is doing his best."

Augusta cast a sideways glance at Lance to see if her sarcasm was finding its mark.

"You're saying that the voters are questioning my performance," said Lance flatly. Marriage had already taught Augusta that Lance reacted unpredictably to criticism and took care not to accuse him directly, playing the role of a sympathetic wife bringing bad news to her faultless husband.

"The voters are blaming you for things you could neither have known nor controlled. Like the bomb that went off in the World Trade Center, the Mississippi River floods and those California forest fires. Even last winter's blizzard, for Christ's sake."

"And your point is?" asked Lance, on the defensive.

"I wish I knew," said Augusta, seemingly perplexed by it all. "The polls say we're in trouble. The media all of a sudden keeps tripping us up and even our one-time friends are disconnecting. They say you play too much golf. I heard someone say Congress is haywire, and progressives and minority groups are calling the shots, leaving you on the sidelines."

"Are they saying I've lost control?"

"I don't know what they're saying but personally, I think we need change, big change, highly visible, drastic change."

She had Lance's complete attention. "Such as?"

"Ummm, I don't know," said Augusta, tapping her lip. "Have you decided who your running mate is going to be this time?"

It took Lance a moment to catch on. "You mean —"

"I mean maybe you need a new face on the home team. Maybe even a Republican."

"But Max is already the Vice President, honey," said Lance, his mind racing. "He's to be my running mate."

"Life can be strange," mused Augusta. "Something might happen. Perhaps he'll decide he has other pressing concerns."

After a long moment, Lance looked up at her. "Maybe," he said, a smile dawning on his face. "Maybe this is exactly the right time for a little junket – thrown by the Allworthy Foundation."

The Junket

Vice President Maxwell Donahue, relaxing in the luxurious front seat of the private Gulfstream V, downed his third Tanqueray martini. Ah, the perks of high office.

As the aircraft banked to the south, the San Jacinto mountains came into view to the west. The sprawling lush Coachella Valley lay ahead with the Palm Springs Airport now visible.

It was most unfortunate that the President had had to pull out of the trip at the last minute. Donahue had tried to reach him but was told the President was not to be disturbed; FLOTUS, likewise, had taken suddenly ill. Donahue took charge, assuming without being told that it was now up to him to make sure everyone had a memorable weekend. The cause was world hunger and raising money to support the cause required outings like this, where the wealthy were shown a good time for a few days. Everyone would bond over drinks, locker room talk, bikini-clad women and sumptuous food. Later, big checks would be signed.

"Our hotel is only three miles from the airport," Donahue announced over the loudspeaker to the tipsy passengers who made up the inner circle of President Lance's White House political aristocracy.

"There it is!"

The passengers scrambled to the plane's windows for a peek. Oohs and aahs of awe and anticipation followed.

"This is paradise, babe," noted one of the more vocal and boozed-up female passengers. "POTUS has no idea what he's missing."

"We're heading to the Parker Meridien resort," Donahue continued. "It's a swanky utopia in the middle of the desert."

The place sat on 13 acres of landscaped gardens, criss-crossed with meandering paths straight out of *Alice in Wonderland*. A sensual playground with sufficient privacy to allow guests so inclined to misbehave and get away with it.

"Four heated swimming pools, ladies and gentlemen, three world-class restaurants and a posh spa — all hiding behind those ivy-covered walls and hedges."

There was applause and hooting. "More seriously though, folks," Donahue continued, reminding himself of what he thought was the real purpose of all this, "our trip has a noble purpose. The President calls it 'humanitarian travel'. I have blocked time to talk about hunger —"

"Heck, I'm already hungry!" someone shouted.

"And we want to discuss do-able solutions, and of course, resources and funding —"

"I could do with a few resources from the nearest bar right about now," said someone else.

The charter jet landed gently and the doors swung open to southern California's signature clear skies and a warm breeze. The resort's top brass waited in line on the tarmac. Donahue apologized for the President's absence.

"Happy hour begins at 6," said Donahue as everyone headed towards their rooms. "The President's instructions were whatever you want and as much as you want."

By 7, the raucous gathering was well lubricated and celebratory. A bacchanalian spirit filled the air around the circular marble poolside bar with a stunning mountain view in every direction. Bottles of top-shelf crafted gins and vodkas and aged single malt whiskeys sat like soldiers on duty. The menu of specialty cocktails alone was three pages long.

"You could buy a nice Learjet for what this bar bill's gonna be," slurred Lance's press secretary, who had strategically left his wedding ring in his room. "A really nice Learjet!"

The next morning Maxwell Donahue washed down four Ibuprofen tablets with a bottle of beer from his mini-fridge. He massaged his throbbing temples as he strained to recall the details of the night before. There had been noise, that he could remember. Anyone even halfway sober trying to sleep would have had to wait until dawn for sufficient quiet. Screams, raucous laughter, cries of passion or perhaps fear had filled the corridors of the long hall of executive suites. Doors had slammed open and shut through the night.

"Where have you been all my life, pretty young thing?"

"Don't touch me!"

"Come back here, you bitch!'

"Stop that, you animal!"

"How dare you!"

Maxwell did remember having opened his door a sliver, surprised by the backs of two naked men chasing one of the housemaids down the hall.

According to the housekeeping superintendent the following morning, jets of champagne had damaged some fine and expensive draperies. The pool attendant spoke of leopard panties and several condoms clogging the pool's filter. Puddles of drying red wine and vomit surrounded the bar.

The summons from the Oval Office took Donahue by surprise, coming as it did almost immediately after his return from the debauchery in the desert. Perhaps POTUS was anxious to know how much money he had raised.

"You and the First Lady sure missed a very special time, Mr. President," he said, as he entered the office. Lance sat behind the Resolute desk, his expression serious.

"Take a seat, Max."

Something was off, Donahue could tell. "Is everything okay, Lance?" he asked, concerned. "Is Augusta —"

"Augusta is fine. About you, though, I'm not sure, my friend, not sure at all. I heard about your little pleasure jaunt to the desert. I must confess it took me a little by surprise."

Donahue was speechless for a moment. "But — but — I was told it was your trip. They said you had to opt out at the last minute because the First Lady had taken ill —"

"I'm not sure who you've been talking to, Max," said Lance evenly. "The First Lady has been fine and so have I."

"That's a relief," said Donahue.

Lance's voice softened. "You and I, buddy, I know we go back a long way. You've always had my back and you know I have appreciated your great work and sacrifices for the party and our administration. We have no secrets — right?"

"Right," said Donahue, not sure where this was heading.

"You know I like my golf and other little pleasures, nothing wrong with that. We're carrying the weight of the world's most powerful nation. And you're entitled to your own downtime too — though I must confess I had no idea you were into threesomes. Naughty boy!" Lance winked conspiratorially.

"But, Lance —"

"Shhh, we're all grown men here, your secrets are safe with me," said Lance. "I just wish you hadn't used $300,000 of Foundation money for your private binge, Max. That's not going to look good when the media finds out."

"But Lance, it was Augusta's idea," said Donahue. "She said you wanted to give some of our major donors a good time and said I could pay for it with Foundation funds."

Lance gave his Vice President a long, level look. "I'll just assume that was a joke, Max. Neither of us had any idea you were doing this. Dragging the First Lady into this is a low blow. I sincerely hope you're not trying to scapegoat my wife. That would be a very poor move, Max."

"But Lance —"

"You need to man up, Max. Someone from the *Washington Post* has already called wanting official confirmation that the Veep had indeed used charity money for a wild personal pleasure junket."

Donahue was breaking out in an anxious sweat, his fingers trembling.

"I think we can handle this one, Max, I don't want you to stress," Lance said in a gentler voice. "I must confess, though, that this could look very bad for the party if it came out while we're on the campaign trail. You know how the White House is full of whistleblowers looking for publishing deals."

Donahue looked morose. "I'm so sorry, Lance. This is a huge misunderstanding. And I have nothing but respect and admiration for Augusta."

"Good, glad to hear that. Anyway, we need to deal with the fallout. This could be a PR nightmare from hell."

"If it comes out."

"Let's just assume it's a matter of time."

Donahue looked down, waiting for the hammer. "What do you suggest, Mr. President?"

"That's your decision, Max," said Lance, standing up to signal the end of the meeting. "You know that whatever you decide, even if you should decide to leave the White House, you will have my full support. That's what friends are for. I know I can count on you to do what's best for the party."

Donahue stood up to leave, looking dejected.

"Cheer up, Max!" the President called after him. "Life doesn't end when you leave the White House, you know."

The announcement came a week later. The President seemed downcast and somber as he looked around the table at his Cabinet. The Vice President's chair was empty.

"I think all of you realize that this is an especially sad day for me. Vice President Donahue and I go back a long way. He was an outstanding American, a great family man and a perfect gentleman with unequivocal integrity. In the time that he served this administration, he has given his office, his party and his country his very best. I personally will miss him deeply. He has been called away by pressing circumstances and has requested that his privacy be respected in the days that follow."

An awkward silence followed. Lance's inner circle had been picked for their unconditional loyalty and unwavering support even under awkward circumstances. Everyone at the table understood the consequences of stepping out of line or betraying the President's trust.

Lance broke the clumsy hush. "I have been giving much thought to Donahue's successor and after much deliberation, I have settled on a name I believe all of you will be able to get behind. I believe none of you will disagree when I say that Samuel Steele is the single most qualified individual for this position — even though he comes from across the aisle. As CIA Director for three years, his work in safeguarding our national security is unsurpassed. Under his leadership, we have made great strides toward better understanding the country's enemies. He has surrounded himself with extraordinarily talented people and made our nation safer. Now, as Vice President, he will continue his work in the international arena while applying his skills to pressing domestic issues."

Heads nodded in agreement.

"We spoke this morning. As I expected, he agreed to step up to the plate. Gentleman, we have a new Vice President!"

The American people spoke the following November. The team of Allworthy and Steele emerged victorious, and by a generous margin. With that, America remained in the hands of an increasingly inscrutable president who seemed to have rescued his stumbling political career by hitching his wagon to a better man from another party.

Different Pleasures

Lance liked the idea. A grand four-week tour of America's important Pacific Rim partners, Singapore, Hong Kong and a final stop in South Korea to warmly congratulate a president who had made it clear that his country was a friend and ally of the US. Augusta had suggested a side trip to Honolulu for R&R; Lance had readily agreed.

The red carpet had already been rolled out to the mobile gangway of Air Force One, sometimes referred to as the 'mansion in the sky'. The President and Augusta were surrounded by a farewell gathering and a cadre of Secret Service agents scoping the area for possible suspicious activity. Thirty-six passengers and 18 crew were already aboard.

Final hugs and handshakes were well under way when Cleo stepped out of the small crowd and unexpectedly faced Augusta, holding out a single long-stemmed rose and a bottle of what looked like champagne. The two embraced somewhat awkwardly.

"Be safe. Enjoy," Cleo said, turning away almost as though she didn't want the First Lady to see her expression.

The front of the plane was filled with friends, hand-picked members of the press, as well as speechwriters, interpreters and security personnel. The midsection housed a large seating area, a cafeteria and galley, as well as sleeping quarters and restrooms. The rear primarily served presidential purposes, including a conference room and a high-tech communications center with a bank of telephones and TV monitors. Beyond were the President's living quarters, consisting of a comfortable sitting area, a large bedroom and a spacious bath.

The President and the First Lady mingled with their guests over drinks and a hot meal. Eventually, as Air Force One banked and headed westward, lights were dimmed and shades pulled down as guests retired to their quarters.

Pulling off his tie and kicking off his shoes, Lance flopped his muscular frame onto the king-sized bed and let out a sigh of relief. On the bedside table stood two long-stemmed glasses and a stainless steel ice bucket monogrammed with the presidential seal. Nestling among the ice cubes was Cleo's gift of a bottle of French champagne. As he worked the cork, Lance said, "How unusually thoughtful of my sister."

"Perhaps an olive branch?" said Augusta.

Lance poured two flutes of the bubbly and took a long swallow, smacking his lips. Augusta set her glass on the table, kicked off her black patent leather pumps and slid off her tailored, dark slacks. Now, clad only in her lacy underwear, she took a long sip of champagne.

Entering the spacious bathroom, featuring Italian marble, Augusta announced, "I think I'll enjoy Cleo's gift while soaking in the tub."

While listening to the bathtub fill up with water, Lance poured himself another flute of champagne, undressed, and flopped down on the satin bed covers atop a mound of large pillows. Almost at once, he began to feel the glow from the champagne. He noticed for the first time the quiet hum of the Boeing turbos powering westward at 500 miles per hour.

Well over half an hour passed before Augusta emerged from the bathroom. Her hair was pinned up. Holding an empty glass in her hand, she faced her husband. His face was flushed from the fizzy.

Augusta was stunning in her total nakedness. Up to this point in their relatively young marriage, their sex life had been unusual, characterized by its almost complete absence. Even on their wedding night they had drunk too much and just collapsed into a deep sleep without even taking off their clothes. The few other times they had attempted sexual intercourse it had consistently ended in frustration and embarrassment. Lance could not even remember the last time the two of them had ventured into the awkward realm of anything that might be considered romantic.

How differently indeed the outside world perceived the President and First Lady. Their inescapable visual appeal had already leaked into the sensual bloodstream of America and the civilized nations across the globe. To anyone watching, this couple epitomized the perfect union but in truth, it was all a lie. The sad reality was that when it came to sex, despite a public veneer of romantic perfection, Augusta and Lance lived physically separate lives.

But tonight, Lance opened his arms.

"Come," he said softly,

Without a word, Augusta slid delicately under the smooth sheets and they embraced. The warm bath and the champagne made what was to come next most uncommon but somehow inevitable. But within a minute, Lance lost control and squandered his release all over Augusta's belly. He pounded the soft pillow next to him with his fist, moaned and slid onto his side with his back toward Augusta.

Then something unusual happened. Instead of also turning away from him, Augusta slid closer and wrapped her arms around him, spooning skin to skin. Perhaps this would account for Lance's condition the next morning. Much to Augusta's surprise, Lance seemed fully aroused and ready to try again. This time was different, perhaps because he was more relaxed. After several glorious minutes,

Augusta rejoiced in Lance's robust and complete ejaculation inside her.

Breathless and delighted, all she could manage to say was, "My, my, Mr. Superman, my, my."

While Augusta basked in the memory of Lance's unexpected performance, another woman, equally wistful, recalled a slightly different kind of pleasurable event.

"May I ask you something?" Sam had said.

Karissa remembered feeling nervous about what Sam's question might be. Would this finally be a more intrusive interrogation into her past? Something about her work performance?

What came instead was a surprise. "May I request the pleasure of your company at the annual White House Easter Egg Roll two weeks from now? As my plus one?" he had asked. Karissa found herself visiting and revisiting the memory of the day with pleasure.

The weather had been spring-like. The south lawn of the White House was a lush green with its southern magnolias ready to pop and the traditional surrounding tulips bordered by grape hyacinth now in full bloom. The air was fresh and fragrant. Karissa remembered spending an unusual amount of time deliberating on what to wear. Keenly aware that the attendees might include not only the vice president but also other important guests and the TV networks with all their viewers, how much of her smooth, ivory skin would be appropriate to expose, she wondered?

She settled on a below-the-knee cotton sundress with a pastel floral design. Spaghetti straps exposed bare shoulders but no cleavage. She carried a light lavender sweater in case the afternoon turned cool.

Karissa had clearly chosen well. Several times throughout the festivities, she caught the Vice President stealing glances at her.

"How lovely you look," he said on several occasions throughout the afternoon.

The atmosphere was joyful, and Karissa happily immersed herself in the events of the afternoon. There were children laughing everywhere, a competition with colored eggs, a delicious sponge cake and a fruit punch from the White House kitchen. A blur of festive feelings and romantic innuendo.

There was a moment when her mind had stepped back and cruelly reminded her – *Here you are, a Lebanese Muslim, a child of war, an American under false pretenses*. Her heart now pounded as the special guest of the Vice President of the United States.

"Thank you so much for attending, Ms. Smithson," Steele's voice broke into her ruminations. "It was such a pleasure to have you here. I have arranged for a White House limo to take you safely home."

Karissa remembered saying, "Thank you so much — that's very thoughtful of you, sir." A small wave of disappointment washed over her that the afternoon was ending until Steele leaned in and whispered, "Not sir, please. Just Sam."

"Will we run this Sunday — Sam?" she asked, as he opened the limo's rear door and helped her in, their fingers touching briefly.

"Hmmm," said Steele, as though solving a knotty problem. "Will we stop for a pastry?"

"Yes!" she said, flirting back.

"You won't mind my herd of Secret service bodyguards?"

"Ummm," she pretended. "I'll tolerate them."

"In that case," said Steele, "yes, we will run!"

Plan B

Dressed in blue hospital scrubs, Chief Pathologist Dr. Cleo Allworthy surveyed the underground morgue at the Walter Reed Medical Center. The sunless space reminded her of a fox's den and was a curious source of comfort to her. Being alone in her cocoon suited her; she preferred the solitude and a pack of cigarettes.

Approaching the porcelain-topped table, she read the clinical summary appended to the cadaver's toe tag —

"42-year-old male with a 4-month-old history of progressive agitation, memory loss, confusion, dysfunctional speech and loss of coordination. Cause of death: acute aspirational pneumonia."

Unusual. Too young, she thought.

Cleo reminded herself that there were no absolute

truths in pathology. Not all hoof beats came from galloping horses; a zebra could show up when you least expected it. And she had an idea why this particular male had died so young.

Putting on her apron and surgical gloves, she secured the headpiece that protected her face with a clear plastic shield. There was work to be done.

The vibrating bone saw made short work of both sides of the ribcage, allowing her to remove the heart and lungs. Cleo eyed the empty body cavity, which always reminded her of the hull of an ancient ship under construction.

She made a circular cut around the equator of the cranium. A soggy aggregate of bone, blood, skin and cerebrospinal fluid splattered against her plastic face mask and apron.

The first knock, knock, went unnoticed.

Just as she lifted off the bony cap of the skull to expose the brain, there was another impatient hammering on the door. Lance's voice came through — "Should I make a new appointment for some suitable time in the next millennium, Dr. Allworthy?"

"I'm coming, I'm coming." With irritation in her voice, Cleo hurried across the morgue and unlocked the door. "You're early!"

Lance turned ashen and steadied himself against the door. Cleo looked terrifying. As though her blood-splashed autopsy uniform was not enough, her face was partly obscured by the human detritus clinging to her face shield.

"You look like a Halloween monster."

Cleo hastily removed her face gear, peeled off her gloves and untied her apron, stuffing everything into a nearby bin marked 'Biohazard'. As color returned to Lance's face, so did his tone of presidential arrogance.

"What can I say? My visit to cheer up the wounded warriors upstairs went quicker than I had anticipated. ABC News got their video and a sound bite from me and it was all over."

Cleo retrieved the vial of Lance's allergy serum from the refrigerator.

"What if those brave soldiers upstairs who shed their blood for our country knew what a wimp their president was? Afraid of a teensy needle!"

Cleo plunged the needle into his left deltoid.

"I'm coming back to the White House with you today," she announced firmly as she squeezed the syringe's contents into him.. "It's been months since I've seen Augusta."

"First Ladies have a lot of things to do, you know. She's just being a good First Lady."

"But why no word from her for so long? Why do I feel all is not well?"

"I'll tell her you asked about her," Lance said, pushing back against the idea of Cleo visiting.

"That will not do," Cleo snapped. "I want to see her face to face. I'll follow in my car."

The sentry on duty at the southeast gate of the White

House inspected Cleo's windshield decal with the White House seal, glanced at her ID card and waved her through. She parked in a visitor slot and entered the building, walking to the elevator that went to the presidential residence.

Lance was already at the door in his workout attire.

"Sorry, sis, can't stay and chat," he said. "Gotta tone me up and then dine with my cabinet."

Augusta emerged from the bedroom. "Oh my god, it's such a joy to see you again, Cleo. It's been forever. You will stay for lunch, won't you, my dear?"

"I'd be delighted," Cleo said.

Augusta looked just as attractive but something about her appearance had changed. Was her face perhaps slightly fuller? Was there a rosy glow about her? Shinier hair? She looked a few pounds heavier in her fitted, cashmere sweater, her bosom ampler than Cleo remembered.

And then there was the unmistakable bump.

"Augusta!" Cleo's hand flew to her mouth. "Are you—?"

"Pregnant." Augusta's eyes moistened up, her cheeks flushed. "Six months."

Cleo waited for an expression of joyous motherhood that did not come.

"It's a boy." A deep sob broke free from Augusta.

"The day the doctor told us the child would have Down's syndrome," said Augusta, her voice sinking to a barely audible whisper. "That was when —"

"Oh my god, Augusta," said Cleo, opening her arms and pulling the First Lady into a hug. "I had no idea. I can't begin to imagine what you've been through these last months."

Augusta relaxed into Cleo's arms.

"You know him as well as I do, Cleo. Lance has always been about perfection."

Cleo nodded, "He would see a child with Down's as defective and a mark of shame."

Augusta stepped back from the hug. "No, Cleo," she said. "Down's or not, Lance never wanted to be a father."

"So?"

"He insisted I get an abortion."

"That cold bastard!"

"I told him I would divorce him before I would terminate the pregnancy."

"I'm sure he'd have none of that," said Cleo. She knew her thin-skinned brother would never dare risk the scandal of a failed marriage.

"Lance wants to keep me out of the public eye as much as possible. The baby is to be born without fanfare, thousands of miles away. In Sudan of all places."

Cleo's heart sank. "Sudan — isn't that where Princess Diana used to visit Africans suffering from leprosy and AIDS?"

"Yes. Lance wants to set up a similar low-profile humanitarian cover for me. I'll ostensibly be helping with the

Allworthy Foundation's war against hunger."

Cleo asked, with concern, "Are you afraid?"

"The Sudanese are apparently friendly and polite. I expect they'd be respectful of an American dignitary's privacy, even without knowing she was the First Lady. So no, I'm not overly worried."

Cleo placed her hand on Augusta's swollen belly, caressing, sensing the life within. "Well, this little fella is not going to be easy to hide."

"Thought of that too. The baby will be well concealed inside the traditional Sudanese *tobe* — a loose wraparound. And of course a scarf will hide my face."

Cleo was struggling to make sense of the plan.

"After the birth, the baby will come back here with you?"

"No. I'll come back alone."

"I don't understand, Augusta. You mean you'll leave the child to be adopted by —" She was aghast, at a loss for words.

"Shhh, my dear," said Augusta, gently pulling Cleo to her in a full, warm embrace. Everything that followed was unscripted and spontaneous. Augusta cradled Cleo's face in her hands. Their eyes closed before their lips met. The first kiss was brief but the second one lingered. The two pulled apart slowly, both surprised by the intensity of the moment.

"Tell me, Augusta," said Cleo, her voice soft now. "Even if you put the child up for adoption, wouldn't you want to make sure he's cared for by a loving family?"

"And he will be!" Cleo sensed a new timbre in Augusta's voice, akin to the ferocity of a lioness protecting her cubs. "The adoptive parents must be pre-approved by me."

"But how —"

"In fact, I know exactly who they'll be. They just don't know it yet."

Cleo stared at Augusta, dumbfounded.

"And that, my dearest Cleo, is where you come in. Come, we have much to plan."

Meeting Adjourned

Samuel Steele didn't like what he saw going on around him. He wished he could share his observations with someone he could trust. A VP's powers are limited but there was so much that needed attention. Steele knew he had won the election for Lance but now he struggled to support the President's agenda, the specifics of which were elusive and opaque.

"Meeting adjourned," said the President. His cabinet members pushed away from the massive mahogany table in the Situation Room and began leaving, once again confused.

The President had called the meeting but no one was quite clear exactly why. He had rambled on for half an hour about how poorly the White House chef had prepared his meals without the First Lady to draw up the menu.

Steele especially was concerned by the President's unusually unkempt appearance. His suit was rumpled. A large grease spot soiled his blue tie and a dark stubble covered his chin and cheeks. The Vice President stepped forward as Lance stood up. "Is everything all right, Mr. President?"

Lance looked at his watch. "Why, of course," he said, as though put off by the question. "Excuse me now, I don't want to be late for my workout."

The President hurried off, leaving Steele wrestling with the security implications of Lance's curious behavior and appearance. The President was in a job that never let up, where anything could happen, where he needed all his senses about him for that 3 a.m. call that everyone hoped would never come. When anything could happen, Steele knew from experience, it usually did, sooner or later.

Time to deal with it, he thought. And he knew just the people for the job.

Ten years had passed since ET Haynes and Jack Goodwell had bailed from their F-4 fighter jet over Beirut's Marine Barracks. Not surprisingly, success had followed them after they'd left the military and co-founded a security and surveillance systems company with the unassuming name of SURCOM. Together, they represented formidable expertise in image capture technology, digital electronics, fiber optics lens capabilities and infrared communications. Their company quickly became an industry leader, landing one lucrative contract after another.

Inevitably, a number of these contracts involved the federal government. Many government agencies, including the White House, had been in desperate need of upgrading their security and surveillance capabilities, and SUR-COM, with its reputation for integrity, superb service and competitive pricing, became the government's contractor of choice.

ET and Jack met with the President and Vice President on a Monday afternoon. The Vice President had spent 30 minutes before the meeting briefing them on the precise requirements of the White House, particularly the locations that POTUS frequented.

ET and Lance hardly met anymore except during the annual family get-together at Christmas. Their paths had diverged sharply as their careers veered off in different directions. After his marriage, ET had been far too content with Kat and immersed in the new business to have much time left, especially for difficult relationships.

Still, he had never seen Lance at his Oval Office desk and there was a smile of anticipation on his face as they were ushered in.

Lance's eyes passed over ET and Jack without any change of expression.

"Did we schedule a meeting for now, Sam?" he asked the Veep. "And who are these gentlemen?"

"We did, Mr. President," Steele replied. "You wanted a security review —"

"You mean you wanted one," interrupted Lance. His face was stony and still without expression.

"Well, it's long overdue, Lance," Steele said gently. "And these two —"

Lance looked over ET and Jack, still without recognition.

"Who are these two?" he asked.

ET was clearly baffled, with no idea whether Lance was playing a joke or something else was going on.

"SURCOM has been making federal agencies and offices secure for years now, Mr. President. I can't think of anyone I'd be more comfortable with checking out the White House security system and making it state-of-the-art. Let me introduce you though."

Lance raised his hand, silencing Steele and looked directly at ET, his eyes distant and cold.

"I know this guy," he said. "He's a photographer, not a security expert."

"Lance, is this some kind of joke?" asked ET.

Another long stare and then Lance said, "To you, Mr. President, please."

"You — you don't recognize me?" ET asked. "Really?"

Lance sat back in his chair and waved around the room. "Sit down, gentlemen," he said. "Don't loom over the most powerful man on the planet. And you —" he wagged a finger towards Jack — "of course I recognize you."

Everyone waited in silence. Suddenly, the President

burst out laughing.

"Oh my God, ET," he said. "Can't you tell when I'm joking, man? Of course I know who you are. Why would I forget the guy who took those great photos during my Governor campaign?"

Steele interrupted diplomatically. "Mr. President, we need many, many more cameras, brighter lighting on the grounds and motion detectors at strategic points —"

Lance was on his feet, suddenly livid, unrecognizable from a moment earlier.

"We need nothing," he roared, unexpectedly loud, making everyone flinch. "Get out of my room! You're all excused!"

Steele, embarrassed, hustled ET and Jack out of the room. The President's voice followed them out: "And if you want to spy on me, for Christ's sake, don't be so damn obvious about it, Steele!"

Once they were outside the White House, ET looked at Jack, shaking his head. "That was scary," he said. "That isn't the Lance I know. Something is very, very wrong."

A Child Too Far

Dr. Cleo Allworthy never really got over her fear of public speaking but over the years, she had learned to overcome her apprehensions through complete mastery of her subject matter. Her reputation as an expert in cognitive impairment and the various forms of dementia was hard won. That evening's well-attended conference, titled *Diseases of the Mind — What's New?* was at the Marriott Convention Center in downtown Washington.

Cleo took a nervous sip of water and looked out at the audience of neurologists, pathologists, neuroscientists, psychiatrists and a herd of primary care physicians, the first ones most likely to detect the onset of mental decline in their patients.

"We are indeed facing a monster," she told the gathering. "The impact of dementia on modern society is beyond calculation. The economic, social, and cultural consequences are truly immeasurable. There are several kinds of dementia with the commonest being Alzheimer's disease, its definitive diagnosis being confirmed by specific microscopic findings within the brain at autopsy. Sadly, as you all know, there is no cure for this devastating condition at the present time. While Alzheimer's primarily affects the elderly, rarer forms of dementia exist that attack much younger victims, snatching them away while they are in the prime of their lives. We believe that in many cases there is a genetic component that predisposes these unfortunate individuals to manifest the disease early."

Forty minutes later Cleo ended her lecture to cordial applause. Just as soon as she could without drawing attention, she fled the Convention Center and drove away, pointing her Volvo in the direction of Andrews Air Force Base. She did not want to miss Augusta's arrival.

Lance had reluctantly caved to Cleo's insistence that she be present to greet Augusta when her plane landed. But once they reached the airfield, he found an unexpected, and not entirely welcome, surprise — ET and Kat were already there.

"Hello, brother of mine," said Kat cheerily. "Lovely to see you again."

"Greetings, brother-in-law," ET said, rapidly clicking several photos.

"But – how did you two know –" Lance ran out of words.

"Let's just say a little bird from Africa told us," said Kat with a wink.

The airplane lumbered toward its parking spot just 30 yards from where they were standing. Lance's mind was crowded. He was not sure who would be emerging from the plane. It would be Augusta, but would it be the same Augusta who'd left for Africa three months earlier? Did he still mean anything to her? There had been no communication between the President and his wife for 90 days. *I wonder if she even thought about me?* He realized, with irony, that he himself had hardly thought about her except to worry about the child she would bring forth. *What if she were to emerge holding the imperfect child for the world to see? I should have insisted on the abortion.*

"One big happy family," Lance said awkwardly, tapping his foot impatiently.

ET and Kat held hands, smiling, full of anticipation. Their smiles had started the day Cleo showed up at their home with a mysterious smile of her own. She alone knew how much they yearned for a child. Years earlier, Kat had undergone a hysterectomy after being diagnosed with life-threatening hemorrhagic endometriosis. The operation had left her unable to conceive a child. Cleo's gift to them that day was the news that a child would soon be available for adoption, one she knew they would just adore.

As Cleo shared the details of Augusta's solution to her

predicament, Kat could barely hold back her happiness. Of course they'd take the child; of course they would cherish him.

"I think we're going to have Christmas early this year," ET had joked, taking Kat's hand in his.

"There is one other thing you should know about the baby," Cleo had said.

"Whatever it is, that child is going to be ours," said Kat.

Cleo had gently revealed that the coming baby would have Down's syndrome.

There had been a silence while ET and Kat looked at each other.

"Well," ET had said finally. "I think we all know what that means. That child is just going to have to get twice as much love."

Cleo shared the plan in step-by-step detail. ET and Kat would have to apply right away to a certain care center in Sudan, the one where Augusta would leave her child after birth. The care center had kindly agreed to make sure the baby was assigned to the Hayneses.

At the US end, their case would be fast-tracked after receiving a special request from the First Lady. No one would know who the mother of the child in question was.

The plane came to a complete stop and its engines wound down. Five minutes later, a now slender Augusta stepped out carefully, moving down the mobile gangway. Escorted by two

Secret Service agents, she walked toward the waiting group.

She stopped when she was six feet away from them, her expression a mix of relief and complete exhaustion.

"Honey, you have no idea how much I've missed you," Lance stuttered awkwardly, stepping forward with an unwieldy bouquet in one hand to give Augusta a peck on her cheek and not quite a hug.

ET looked at Kat, rolling his eyes, before they both stepped forward to greet Augusta. "We've missed you so much," Kat said, offering Augusta her opened arms.

"Welcome home, Madam First Lady," ET said warmly.

Cleo was the last in line. Moving to Augusta, she said softly, "Welcome home, long-lost traveler." She took her hand in hers, not sure if a hug would give too much away, but then wrapped her arms around her. "God, I've missed you," she whispered into Augusta's ear.

Abruptly, Lance looked at his watch and said, "I wish I could stay, folks, but I gotta run. Important presidential security briefing. Or something. Catch you all later."

He turned on his heel and walked briskly back toward the presidential armored vehicle nicknamed 'The Beast'.

A Home For Bertie

Three weeks later, a privately chartered 7X Whisper Jet with three passengers came to a stop just before midnight at the end of remote runway 19 at Reagan International Airport. The flight from Montréal to Washington, D.C., had taken just less than an hour. The long-haul Turkish Airlines flight from Khartoum to Montréal had also gone smoothly without delays — or media attention.

Cleo jammed another cigarette into the ashtray. Her Volvo was the only car waiting on the tarmac; the other vehicle there was an ambulance with 'Sibley Memorial Hospital' lettered along its side.

Cleo's sedan headlights revealed two uniformed women exiting the aircraft and hurrying toward the ambulance, one carrying a small bundle wrapped in a blanket, the other a large black bag.

Cleo lit another cigarette and smiled.

Tomorrow was going to be a big day.

The near total gridlock was typical for a Washington, D.C. morning. This was exactly why Kat and ET rarely drove anywhere, preferring public transportation. But today was different; today was special. Today a car was absolutely necessary.

They arrived at the entrance to Sibley Memorial Hospital just after 9 a.m., a few minutes late. Holding hands, they made their way past the lobby, finally entering the cluster of administrative offices just left of the gift shop from which wafted the fragrance of fresh flowers and a cluster of 'Get Well Soon' balloons.

"Good morning!" came with a smile from a neatly dressed, middle-aged woman behind a walnut desk in the reception area. "I'm Cindy, Mr. Clarke's executive assistant. You must be the Hayneses. He's expecting you."

She ushered the two past a heavy, rosewood door into the office of John Clarke, head of the hospital's Legal Department. He was a big man with a round red face, dressed in a white, button-down shirt with sleeves rolled up and a sporty Ivy League striped bowtie.

Mr. Clarke gently clapped his hands together to bring the meeting to order. "Good morning, Mr. and Mrs. Haynes. Please do sit down." He offered the happy pair a broad smile. "I know you're anxious to get on with the day's business."

He looked like a beardless Santa Claus, his tone celebratory, almost joyous. Numerous discharge documents were waiting to be signed and Clarke dwelt on each, translating the legalese into simple English for the Hayneses, who nodded and signed wherever he pointed.

Half an hour went by quickly.

"All right, then, I do believe we are done here. My congratulations to both of you. Master Bertram Haynes is a lucky young man!"

Clarke stood and they shook hands again. "Cindy will take you upstairs to the nursery. They're waiting for you."

In the nursery's bright and cheery lounge, Augusta and Cleo stood as the elevator door opened and ET and Kat stepped out. The four converged, arms wide open. Tears and joy, both flowed together.

"Augusta, this I promise," said Kat. "We will give him the best life he could possibly have."

"I know you will," said Augusta. "That's why I chose you. I am not giving up Bertram. I'm placing him in your hands, knowing he will be loved and cherished forever under your care."

The young nurse greeted the foursome in the waiting room, and then addressed Kat and ET. "The doctors have checked your child from head to toe — and found him physically fit to travel home with you today."

ET squeezed Kat's hand.

Augusta turned towards the elevator. "Well, there it is. It's official now," she said. "I'm going to leave you to it."

"That's my cue to leave, I think," said Cleo, also rising.

The nurse led ET and Kat down the hall into a nursery painted light blue.

"Presenting — your son!" The nurse's hand touched the foot of the baby-blue bassinet. Little Bertram, wearing a blue stocking cap, was sleeping soundly. He had the expected but subtle Mongoloid features but the angelic face was filled with warmth and calm. Kat and ET looked down at the child that as of this day was legally theirs. The nurse gently placed the baby in Kat's arms.

ET leaned in towards the infant and whispered, "Welcome home, Bertram Haynes."

"Bertie," Kat said smiling.

"Bertie it is!"

Intensive Care

"Cowboy! I'm home!"

Katherine Haynes, back from church, dropped her purse on the kitchen counter.

"A peck on the cheek for the love of my life," ET called back from the living room.

Kat looked past him to the Christmas tree she and ET had decorated the day after Thanksgiving while Bertie watched from the high perch of his baby seat on the dining room table. As expected, the first few months of Bertie's life had been a love fest. ET and Kat had smothered him with boundless parental affection at every opportunity. They could swear he was even beginning to smile back, which the doctors said was unexpected for his age, given his diagnosis.

"He's stirring from his nap," Kat said.

ET clapped his hands. "Some lunch then and we'll be off for some exercise and a swim!"

That chilly Sunday afternoon, the aging capital YMCA was deserted. Flaking white paint and a maze of antiquated plumbing surrounded the periphery of the Olympic-sized pool. Out of sight somewhere, ancient, cast-iron, steam-filled radiators hissed and thumped. As part of their fitness routine, Kat and ET relished the opportunity to swim and exercise, and when Berty came into their lives, they brought him along, setting him up in a portable carrier so he could watch them splashing about the pool. Not yet six months, sometimes Bertie enjoyed being gently swirled around in the warm water.

Returning home that afternoon, Kat and ET parked the blue bassinet under the Christmas tree so that ET could take a picture of Baby Bertie alert and curious. His eyes flashed at the glitter of tinsel and colored lights above him.

"As if fresh from a manger," Kat said, eyes wet with pride.

ET, not above a manly tear now and then himself, reached for Kat's hand as the two stared down at their little bundle of sheer happiness.

There was a magical connection between the three. And the joy of Christmas matched the moment perfectly.

The horror began five days later — the fever, the difficulty breathing, the obvious distress. Doctors said it was something called Legionnaires disease. People with compromised immune systems could get infected from germs in the air from old air-conditioning.

Or contaminated water in an ancient swimming pool.

The bright spotlights surrounding the White House captured the shape of a dark gray Volvo entering the rear gate. After receiving perfunctory salutes from the pair of armed marines at the gate, the vehicle was waved on.

Cleo plunged another cigarette into the stuffed ashtray protruding from the dash as she looked for the nondescript doorway marked 'Delivery Entrance'.

A door opened and a uniformed attendant appeared, raising his arms to signal that he recognized the approaching vehicle. The First Lady, in a tailored, beige raincoat emerged, a woolen scarf cocooning her face. As the attendant held the door open, she entered the sedan where Cleo awaited her.

"How is he?" she whispered. "Any good news?"

"I heard from Kat an hour ago. He is now in intensive care. They can't seem to get the fever down or stabilize his breathing. His oxygen level keeps dropping. They're debating a tracheotomy."

"Tracheotomy?"

"Surgically creating an opening in his windpipe to connect him to a machine that will breathe for him, pushing oxygen into his lungs."

Augusta's head sank.

Cleo reached out for her hand and squeezed. "We should be there in less than half an hour," she said gently.

A chill rain began to lash Washington, D.C., obscuring the windshield as the sedan sped north.

Twenty minutes later, the vehicle turned into the doctors' parking lot of Walter Reed Medical Center, its wipers still arcing to and fro. Sharing an umbrella, the two women dashed through the hospital's massive front entrance, registered at the front desk and donned surgical masks before entering the so-called rotunda, a large, circular space where each critically ill patient was a spoke in a wheel whose hub housed the nurses and doctors stations.

Augusta and Cleo approached the bedside cautiously, looking down at the frail child. The sight was as chilling as the rain outside. A slender tube led into his windpipe, hissing rhythmically to the pumping of the mechanical respirator. Multiple intravenous lines snaked into the inert child, carrying fluid medications. His limbs were restrained so that these lifelines could function undisturbed but they effectively shackled the child to his bed. The sound from a bank of noisy monitors hummed nearby. The air was heavy with apprehension and the odor of bleached sheets and industrial strength disinfectant.

A nurse brought water and cookies for the four people in vigil around the child's bed.

"Do you think he'll come?" Kat asked Augusta anxiously. They both knew who she was referring to. From the time the child had been brought on to American soil, Lance had neither visited him nor once asked after him.

"I don't know, Kat," said Augusta, her voice heavy with regret. "I think Lance considers his public image more precious than the life and health of his own child."

Kat and ET stared at each other, stunned by the words the President's wife had just spoken.

ET broke the mood by standing up. "I'm going to call Lance myself," he announced. "He needs to be here now!"

Chatter Matters

There had been a striking uptick in the level of terrorist chatter during the first week of December, a rise so dramatic that Karissa's schedule had become almost inhuman.

Most of the chatter had been coming from within the vast area between North Africa and the Middle East, including Afghanistan, Egypt, Yemen, Saudi Arabia, Iran, the mountainous regions of west Pakistan and, of course, Lebanon. But in recent weeks, there had been a disconcerting increase in the volume of terrorism-related electronic chit-chat originating within the United States. The density was highest in the corridor between the District of Columbia and Baltimore, Maryland.

A week earlier, this observation had led to a special briefing session to which Karissa had been invited. Those present included top officials from the National Threat Assessment Center, the directors of the NSA, the CIA and the FBI, Vice President Steele and a seemingly disinterested President Allworthy.

The presentation laid out increasingly worrisome evidence of a threat to the capital region and closed with a review of defensive and offensive strategies already in place. Recommendations were made on the state-of-the-art surveillance technology available for tracking and intercepting the bad actors.

Seated towards the rear, Karissa raised her hand. While some of those present might have considered it above her station as a mere translator to speak up, she did so anyway. "How many of those micro-tracking devices are currently in use?"

Vice President Steele, facing Karissa, answered the question. "Only a few at this time."

"So the situation is not under control?" Karissa asked.

"I'd have to say no. The threats remain very real. It's just not possible to predict every terrorist attack with our current technological capabilities."

The meeting had lasted almost an hour. The President's attention had sometimes wandered off. His few interjections suggested a less than total grasp of what had been shared.

"Thank you, gentlemen and, er, ladies." He looked down at the table as though searching for words. His hands played with a bottle of mineral water.

"Has anyone tasted this stuff they're calling water?" He held up the bottle. "Tastes like ditch water to me."

He turned to Steele. "Hey, you're supposed to be the Veep. Can't you do something about this? I'd have thought a high-level group like this should get something more classy, right? Maybe a good old malt whiskey?"

There was a stunned silence in the room. Finally, to break the mood more than anything else, Karissa raised her hand again, and Lance nodded at her to speak. She stood and faced the group.

"Vice President Steele has asked me to play for all of you a particular stretch of recurring suspicious chatter from last week's traffic."

Through the overhead speaker system came a familiar melody, the Christmas carol *Oh Come All Ye Faithful*. But what chilled everyone in the room were the lyrics: they were entirely in Arabic.

"It is not unusual for hymns to be sung in other languages, including Arabic," said Karissa. "After all, there are Christians among Arabs too."

"What's your point then?" snapped Lance.

"I believe—" Karissa hesitated. "I believe the choice of this particular hymn at this time of year might represent a jihadist call to action. An anti-Christian, anti-Christmas, anti-American attack may be imminent." She paused a moment before adding, "I hope I'm wrong."

From the side of the room, an aide approached the President, leaned down and whispered into his ear.

"Who called?" said the President, not bothering to restrain his voice. "I don't know any Ernest."

The aide bent and whispered again.

"ET Haynes? Well, damn. Who's that?"

Another whisper, longer this time.

The President seemed confused. "So there is an ET Haynes. His son Bertram Haynes is sick. Did I get that right?"

The aide, now standing at attention, said, "Yes, sir."

"And I should know this why?"

The aide, not bothering to whisper any more, said, "Mr. Haynes said he was your brother-in-law. He said Bertram was in critical condition and you might want to know."

The President's gaze wandered off, landing finally on Karissa. He stared at her for a long moment, as though trying to figure out exactly where he had seen her before. Then he snapped his fingers, remembering.

"Did I just hear you speak of an anti-Christian attack?" he said slowly, enunciating each word.

Karissa began answering, "I'm sorry, Mr President, I —"

"And are you a Christian?"

"Sir, I'm —"

"Aren't you one of those damn Muslims?"

Total silence.

"I am, sir."

The president stood up and pointed a quivering finger directly at Karissa. "Well, look, bitch, you can take your terrorist garbage and get your sorry Arab ass out of here. And I mean now!"

You could have heard a pin drop.

"And the rest of you — dismissed!" shouted Lance.

Baltimore, Maryland

1997

The Site

The unseasonably warm evening had brought out a swarm of ravenous patrons. A line snaked out the door of the recently opened Middle Eastern restaurant and the smell of shawarma and falafel filled the air in front of the so-called Mulakat Café. The thriving eatery with indoor and outdoor seating was the beneficiary of the 1996 revival of the neighborhood along the southern end of Reisterstown Road just north of Baltimore.

After two decades of social and structural deterioration, this unique part of town, a bustling example of American prosperity in the 1950s, was making a comeback supported by a new generation of young, moneyed professionals who had sensed the area's potential. The shells of shut-down shops and grocery stores as well as boarded-up apartment buildings that had once housed affluent Jewish immigrants were among the many structures being renovated or replaced. High-dollar boutiques and upscale restaurants were springing up, mixed with office complexes and banks ready to finance even more commercial restoration projects.

One of these projects was the Mulakat Cafe, from the Arabic word for 'meeting'. As the shuffle of customers going in and out affirmed, this little hotspot appealed to a spectrum of generations. The yuppies were well represented as they cautiously explored a cuisine quite unlike the McDonald's and Howard Johnson's they were used to. More at home were the worldly baby boomers, whose higher level of culinary sophistication already included couscous, doner kebabs and deep-fried hummus. Most at home were the raucous Arabs, whose voices rang the loudest.

In charge of this bustling, cosmopolitan venue was a couple in their mid-thirties, clearly of Middle-Eastern descent. They moved busily from the long outdoor bar to the kitchen, ferrying drinks, eats and Arabic good cheer. It was well-known that they came from wealthy families. Two years earlier, they had bought from the city of Baltimore a pair of deserted brownstones just south of their restaurant for the price of one dollar, with a promise to restore them to their original architectural glory.

The progress of the renovations was an ongoing subject of conversation at the restaurant and the bartender clearly had the latest details. Today's update was that the surrounding neighborhood had been almost completely rehabilitated and attention was now turning to the so-called 'Brownstone Row' consisting of twelve almost identical side-by-side structures that represented the most challenging and costly final phase of the reconstruction project. The interiors of each brownstone unit would be gutted before the façades were rebuilt. Trucks delivered construction materials and hauled away debris daily.

At the end of the long outdoor bar with its colorful counter done up with a Middle-Eastern mosaic of tinted glass, a large figure slouched on a high bar stool, a steaming meal of kebabs with pickled cucumbers, baba ghanoush and a fresh tabbouleh salad in front of him. A small dog, a genetic mishmash of cocker spaniel with golden brown spots, sat attentively at his feet. The man, with a snow-white beard and thinning hair barely concealed by a yarmulke, seemed both at ease and intrigued by the busy air and noises of the café.

"Here you go, Penny girl," he murmured, slipping his four legged compatriot a hot kebab. "Another hand-me-down."

The bartender cut a large wedge of lime, dropped it into the ginger ale and slid the glass toward the old man. "Here you go, sir," he said. "Another ginger ale for you." He asked, more as an afterthought, "You don't like spirits?"

The old man shook his head, "Nah, you?"

Before the bartender could reply, the old man's attention was captured by four Middle Eastern men who were heading straight to an outside table some five feet from where he sat at the end of the bar. The bartender recognized them with a wave and a few minutes later bowls of some kind of stew and several pieces of stone-fired flatbread appeared.

Two of the men looked scruffy and in need of a good scrubbing. As they passed him, the old man had caught a whiff of stale perspiration, curry and burnt rubber. The elbows of their faded gray shirts were worn thin. Their dirty, loose-fitting trousers and mud-caked sandals matched their grimy fingernails. They got right down to the business of eating without utensils, pushing the stew about the bowl with pieces of bread. Their contribution to the conversation was limited to the occasional grunt.

The other two men, one in his late twenties and the other in his early sixties, were distinctly different, seeming more refined and better dressed. The younger one wore a pale red woolen skull cap and a neatly pressed white linen tunic, and was clean-shaven but for a manicured horseshoe mustache. A tattoo was visible on the right side of his neck. He ate his meal with clean hands and a spoon. As if sharing a secret, he spoke in hushed tones to the older man who stared at him intently through a pair of dark-rimmed sunglasses. His head was covered with thick gray hair, as were his neck and arms. His salt-and-pepper stubble did not completely cover the severe facial excavations of adolescent acne. He wore a tight, short-sleeved black shirt and dark tapered slacks which highlighted his well-muscled frame.

The old man watching them swiveled his bar stool for a better angle and waited, hoping he might hear something of interest that was not in Arabic, a language unfamiliar to him. Some minutes later his patience was rewarded. He discerned several accented English words and phrases: *Pentecostal Church*, followed by what sounded like *Jesus-loves-you*, spoken like a single word. Twice, he heard someone refer to a house that was white. Interjected a little later within more Arabic came the phrase *Bronie Stone Arrow* from the younger man with the mustache.

The old man wearing the yarmulke, his curiosity aroused now, rose from his bar stool and, Penny in tow, ambled towards the café's entrance like a customer on his way out. As he passed the four men, he paused and turned towards them raising his hand to his chin as though struck by a sudden thought.

"Excuse me, gentlemen," he said, addressing the younger man. "I couldn't help but overhear some of your conversation. I don't understand Arabic, of course, but I heard you use an odd English phrase — a Bronie Stone Arrow. Never heard that one before. I wondered if you might have been referring to the Brownstone Row."

The young man stiffened, his face coloring red. "So?" he said. "It is your business?"

"Not at all," said the old man deferentially. "No offense intended. Just old-fashioned curiosity is all."

The young man abruptly stood up from the table as if

the situation was intolerable. For a moment, he glared at the old man as though daring him to make a move.

"I do hope I did not upset you," the old man said quite amiably. In response, the young man took an aggressive step forward, his foot landing squarely and forcefully on the tail of the poor dog, which had just sat down. Penny yelped in pain. In response, startled and appearing further enraged, the young man kicked the dog, making her yelp even louder.

"What are you doing? She won't hurt you!" the old man shouted, clearly upset, picking up his dog and stepping back.

"Why don't you and your half-breed dog poke your noses somewhere else?" the young man snapped.

The hirsute older man in sunglasses seated at the table had been watching the exchange calmly. He said something sharply in Arabic to the young firebrand, causing him to sit down at once.

Turning now to the man wearing the yarmulke, who was still cradling his dog, he continued, "I apologize for this worthless boy's behavior. Sometimes he forgets his culture — and what did you say your name was, sir?"

The old man considered the question for a few moments, weighing his answer.

"It's Shipley," he said pleasantly. "Ben Shipley."

The hirsute man adjusted his sunglasses, speaking evenly, his voice no louder than before, "Perhaps it's best for you if you get out of here, Shippilee."

The old man looked down at his quivering sidekick then back up at the man behind the dark rimmed glasses, trying to comprehend all that had just happened.

"Come on, Penny girl," he said. "Time to go home."

With that, 'Benjamin Shipley' and Penny hurried away from the Mulakat Café.

All About Saul

Benjamin Shipley wasn't his real name, of course.

Saul Sussman, 82, had quickly realized that he might have disturbed a hornet's nest with his innocent questioning of the four Middle Eastern men at the café. Though he'd faked his name on the spur of the moment, he knew it would be easy for them to find out his real name. After all, he had lived on the tree-lined Brownstone Row overlooking Druid Lake, north of Baltimore, for over 35 years.

He could still recall the excitement when he and his wife had first moved there. In those early days, this first-generation Jewish enclave had been filled with ambitious middle-class aspirations and community spirit. Back then, Brownstone Row used to be considered the most desirable location in the neighborhood.

Then things had changed.

Crime, poverty and drugs had invaded the once-idyllic suburban street. Saul's original neighbors had abandoned Brownstone Row and moved to more secure neighborhoods further north. Saul alone had chosen to stay put. He had just lost his wife and there had been no children. Depressed and weary, he saw no attraction in a new start. He stayed where he was, in his own deteriorating brownstone, suddenly right next door to the bustling renovation project. He had survived on Meals on Wheels and the unwavering affection of his cocker mongrel.

Up until the recent whirr of nearby activity, Saul's existence had slipped into a swamp of boring rituals that blurred the boundary between being dead and being alive. But now, a swell of eager curiosity had captured the old man. The more he thought about it, the more intrigued he was by the unsettling encounter with the four Arabs at the café, especially the hot-tempered young Arab's hostile response to a harmless question. Saul had been even more unnerved by the low-pitched menace of the hirsute older fellow in sunglasses. But what worried him the most was the reference to the 'Bronie Stone Arrow', which he was now certain referred to the Brownstone Row buildings where he happened to live.

"What do you say, Penny girl," he said to his devoted companion. "Shall we do some snooping tonight?"

This particular evening enjoyed ample illumination from a smiling harvest moon. It was uncommonly warm considering that winter was just around the corner. Saul could hear a symphony of noises from the backyard of the construction site less than a block away. Penny, in leadership mode, dragged Saul stumbling out the back door and made her way along the hedgerow of boxwoods to the rear of the property. They took a right and soon stood facing the tightly planked fence topped with razor wire that surrounded the shared backyard of the two mysterious brownstones next door. The fence's design was clearly intended to deny outsiders a peek into whatever was causing the noises emanating from within. In the bright moonlight, Saul studied the seams between the vertical slats of the fence in search of a breach that might provide a peephole.

He found a seam wide enough for the kitchen knife he had brought along. Inserting it, he twisted it clockwise some 90 degrees, separating the boards enough so that he could see what lay beyond.

He frowned, trying to reconstruct the yard's layout from memory. There was, of course, the central barn-like structure that had once housed the boat the former inhabitants had used to sail around Druid Lake. Saul realized he was looking at the closed rear door to the boathouse. From the lights and moving shadows within, he surmised that it was occupied.

"I suppose we're in for a wait, pardner," he whispered to Penny, who gave a soft whine of agreement. "Someone has to emerge sooner or later."

Someone did, a scant five minutes later. From their dimly illuminated profiles and heights, Saul recognized the hot-headed, mustachioed fellow with the tattoo and the sinister older man he'd met earlier at the Mulakat Café.

The Promise Of Paradise

The older man with the sunglasses had been younger then. If he closed his eyes, he could still remember that day in southern Lebanon when he had met the young tunnel digger. He had learned his name later, Ashrafi. A gold coin. And truly, what a treasure he had turned out to be.

The tunnel digger had traveled along with five other aspirants in the rattling wreck of a 1960's Datsun pickup some 40 dusty miles to the Paradise Training Camp in the Bekaa Valley, northeast of Beirut. Upon arrival they had been fed and allowed to wash up before being led to the pre-recruitment 'interview'.

"What have you done for the resistance, Ashrafi?" the older man with sunglasses asked the young fellow.

"I started digging a tunnel," the youth replied. "I dug for

four weeks."

"Only started?" the older man quizzed. "Not finished?"

The interviewee did not reply. His face was tight with bottled rage.

"Well?" said the older man.

"I — I couldn't," he stammered. "They took everything away from me." A tear rolled down his face.

The older man remained impassive. "Everything? And that makes you cry like this?"

The young man bowed his head. Every instant of that day was etched into his memory.

He had been tunneling under the desert for four weeks, helping some Palestinian resistance fighters prepare for a guerrilla attack across the northern border of Israel. The Israeli forces knew well the threat these 'terror tunnels' posed.

It was hard and dangerous work, best done at night. Ashrafi, his back glistening with sweat mixed with dirt, dug by the low light from the oil lamp above his head. He barely noticed the soreness in his arm muscles; the work was important. His goal was to reach, unnoticed, the dense natural forest region just east of the Israeli hillside town of Bizet and establish a sniper's nest there aimed at Israeli civilian activities below.

He had laid down his shovel to catch his breath, when something happened that would change his life forever.

Though ten feet of hard rock separated him from the surface, he could hear the muffled roar of low-flying aircraft. The tunnel seemed to vibrate, raining loose dirt and rock down on him as he scrambled backward to claw his way out.

Twenty miles north, the pair of thundering Israeli Skyhawk fighter jets had unleashed their whistling guided cruise missiles into the old city market of southwest Beirut. When Ashrafi reached there, only rubble and rising smoke remained. The explosions had eviscerated the ancient honeycomb of stalls and shops, leaving the charred remains of people he had lived with all his life. His mother, father and younger brother were among those killed in the brutal bombing.

The young man wandered dazed through the ruins of his parents' stall that had sold spices, herbal remedies and local tobacco. It had been a wretched living, one that had left neither time or money for Ashrafi's hungry, nimble mind to receive any schooling or a foundation for a better future.

He dropped to his knees on the hard ground, his tears mixing with the dirt on his skin, raised his face to the heavens and cried out, in torment, "Ya Allah! Ya Allah!"

That was when he knew that he needed a revenge far more savage and satisfying than digging tunnels would provide. He had heard of a place called the Paradise Training Camp, where shattered boys were turned into ruthless, cold-blooded fighters.

The camp, on the premises of an abandoned elementary

school, stood on fertile land, home to some of the finest opium and hashish in the world. The low-lying adobe clay building, surrounded by several open fields and a few motorable roads, was ideal for outdoor military exercises and vehicular maneuvers. The walls of the old school, once covered with the mural art of innocent children, were now filled with renderings of Allah's paradise for true martyrs, with crystal clear rivers, vast lush gardens and dancing full-breasted virgins.

Ashrafi was mesmerized.

The older man, now his mentor, knew he would be the perfect jihad warrior, smart, strong and filled with hate. And so he was. He quickly mastered English and the 'evils' of the west. He relished the study of Islam. Within him grew a profound contempt for the Christian infidels, his enemies. From the Quran, the budding jihadist learned the merits of self-sacrifice. He assumed a life without fear of consequences.

Twelve weeks was all it took. When the training ended, his mentor did something he had never done before. He removed his sunglasses and shook the hand of his young disciple. On his face was the rare semblance of a smile.

"Know this," he said. "You are the chosen spear of Allah. You are made for great things."

Jesus Loves You

The man who was destined for great things was on his knees on a prayer mat within the brownstone's boathouse, seeking Allah's guidance in the great task ahead of him. Little time remained and there was much preparation still to be done. For a Muslim to feel such a thrill at the thought of Christmas Day felt like a travesty but he knew Allah would be pleased. Did he dare such confidence? The man stood after touching the floor with his forehead one final time. In the low light around him, workers bustled about, speaking in low voices.

Meanwhile, outside the razored-wired fence, two figures were on a mission. The sun had set an hour earlier. Two inches of snow had fallen that day making a white Christmas a real possibility. Saul Sussman and Penny crunched along the newly fallen snow to their secret viewing location.

The light from the three-quarter moon was sufficient. Saul once again rotated his kitchen knife between the slats, spreading them apart. Penny circled in place before settling in at his feet.

"The door is open tonight, Penny girl," Saul said in a barely audible whisper. "Let's have ourselves another look."

This time Saul introduced, through the widest point of separation between the two fence boards, a miniature telescope his wife had once used for bird-watching. As he aimed the instrument at the brightly lit interior beyond the open doors, a dull yellow vehicle came into view. It stood at an angle that gave Saul a clear view of its back and right side. Two men were busy working on it with paintbrushes.

"What's this, Penny, a couple of Picassos?" Saul said softly.

The words 'Druid Hill Laundry' on the rear door were being systematically painted over, clearly to make room for whatever the new owner's company was called. The other worker had just completed new wording on the driver's door and across the upper side panels of the vehicle. The black lettering stood out against the faded yellow base color.

JESUS LOVES YOU
And in larger letters along the long upper side panel —
THE NEW PENTECOSTAL CHURCH

Shaking his head in bewilderment, Saul withdrew the telescope first and then the angled knife. "What in the world — Penny girl?" he whispered.

Just then, Saul discerned a man emerging from the shadows and walking briskly towards them. He was outside the fence and must have come from within one of the brownstones. He held something small and curved; Saul was pretty sure he knew what it was.

"Run, Penny!" Saul shouted. The two took off at a sprint towards their house next door, as fast as an old man with a dog could.

Their getaway was helped along by a fortuitous accident when their pursuer slipped in the snow and fell. Before he could pick himself up, Saul and Penny dashed into their house, running toward the main staircase. A wall of dark wood paneling occupied the space under the stairs. Saul quickly slid a 2' x 3' section of the paneling aside to reveal an opening into a compartment about ten feet square.

"In here," Saul whispered. Penny trotted in compliantly though it was a bit of a squeeze before her master was inside. Saul slid the panel door shut, dead-bolting it from within. The hideaway was a relic from earlier days. In the 1950's anti-Semitism in certain quarters of Baltimore as well as the perceived threat of an atomic explosion had moved more affluent residents to create shelters against any sudden threat.

Leaning over with his hands on his knees, trying to

catch his breath, Saul murmured, "I knew this place would come in handy one day, Penny girl."

Outside, the sound of heavy footsteps drew closer and stopped. An eternity later, they receded. Only then did Saul switch on the flashlight hanging on the wall just inside their new shelter.

The beam revealed a small but adequate room, well stocked with familiar items — batteries, water, some canned goods, several blankets and an inflatable mattress, a battery-operated lantern and even a porcelain chamber pot. His late, beloved wife, now departed for nearly twenty years, had insisted that the "bunker", as she called it, always be kept amply stocked.

"Well, at least we're set for the night, old girl," Saul said. Penny let out a mewl of agreement.

"God bless Mrs. Sussman!"

Out Of Touch

The large windowless Situation Room of the White House was jammed with gloomy officialdom. The President, Vice President, cabinet members and the most important representatives from the Terror Threat Assessment Center were seated around the long table. Karissa Smithson stood just behind the Vice President. The President had swiveled his high-back leather armchair around and was facing the wall. Though no one could see him, he was smiling, humming what sounded like the melody of Jingle Bells. His index finger was gold-digging within his left nostril.

Sam Steele, waiting at the other end of the table, was beginning to realize that his cue from the President to start the meeting might never come. Just as he stood up to call the meeting to order, the President's chair swung around.

"Meeting adjourned," the President said, face grim. The stunned group stared back at the leader of the free world.

"I was just kidding," he said. "Has everyone lost their sense of humor?"

He turned to the Vice President. "Sam, I hope this is not going to be another one of those paranoid diatribes from you and your co-conspirators. It's not easy to run the world when you all keep distracting me at every turn."

The President abruptly returned to humming *Jingle Bells*, looking away into the middle distance.

Sam Steele took charge, quietly and clearly updating everyone on recent findings and the grave threat assessment. Only three days ago over coffee, Karissa had shared with him the urgent need she felt for a stepped-up defense posture in and around the nation's capital.

The President seemed to be tuning in and out of the presentation. Steele paused, looking directly at him. "It's Christmas in America, sir. If Jihadist extremists wanted to hit us hard, this would be the time. The White House and the Pentagon would make perfect ideological targets."

The President looked back with an empty expression.

Steele continued resolutely, addressing the room again. "As of this day and until further notice, the Pentagon, National Security Council, FBI, CIA, the White House police and all 911 emergency dispatchers are on high alert. Any possibly significant information will be reported immediately and directly to my office on our secure hotline.

We are on this 24/7 until I say otherwise."

After almost an hour of high-voltage conversation, the meeting drew to a close. "Any further questions?" said the Vice President. "Mr. President?"

Vice President Samuel Steele stared at the vacant eyes of the most powerful man in the world.

He doesn't get it.

"Mr. President, please understand. In the assessment of our best advisors, this threat is not only real but imminent."

The President glared, seeming angry with everything and everyone for having interrupted his 11 a.m. workout ritual.

"Our surveillance team feels strongly that there is a credible threat —"

The President interrupted, snarling back, "For Christ's sake, Sam, can't you see I'm busy? There's no threat. All is well. Your intelligence experts are out of touch."

Looking confused for a moment, he gazed off to his right, his eyes falling upon the large bust of Winston Churchill perched on a pedestal in the corner of the room. Old Winnie would have understood. His eyes roamed again, this time settling on the attractive face of the woman standing behind the Vice President.

"I recognize you," he said. "You're that Muslim chick. I suppose you agree with this assessment."

"I do, Mr. President," Karissa said.

The President stared at her for a moment, then exploded, spraying spit, "Fucking conspiracy theories everywhere. Just get out of here, all of you!"

The outburst subsided just as abruptly. Lance looked at Steele without expression for a long moment and then said, for the second time that evening, "Meeting adjourned."

Redial

Saul took one last nervous look from the third-floor bedroom window of his brownstone. The partially opened door of the boathouse below allowed him a clear view of the activity surrounding the freshly painted bus.

"They're loading it up with something nasty, Penny girl," he said to the dog standing at his feet, tail quivering. The redlined diesel engine came to life with a roar. "They're testing the engine. I think they're almost ready to go. Maybe we should try 911 one more time, old girl."

His first 911 call had been a disaster. The foolish girl at the other end had just kept asking him his name, on and on like a stuck record. All Saul wanted was to be a good citizen and alert somebody about his suspicions but he sure as hell didn't want to be exposed to the ravenous public on some witness stand later.

"At my age! Meshuggeneh!"

Saul sighed deeply and paused for a moment before tilting his head toward Penny. "I could give them the fake name I gave the Arabs, eh? Now wouldn't that be clever?"

Swallowing the lump in his throat, he picked up the receiver of the rotary phone and with a tremulous index finger dialed the number again.

"9-1-1, please state your emergency." He recognized the voice — it was the same dispatcher. He was clearly in her area code.

"Yes, ma'am, I called you several minutes ago."

"Yes, sir, thank you for calling back. Please don't hang up this time. It sounded important."

"Sure won't, ma'am," said Saul, determined to be more cooperative this time. "What can I tell you?"

"Let's start with your name and location, sir."

"Certainly. The name is Shipley. That's Benjamin Shipley, Ben to friends," said Saul.

As the dispatcher noted the details of Saul's story, her eyes widened with increasing concern about its significance. It all sounded plausible to her now— the Christian bus, the conversation in the café, the menacing Arabs, the strange organic smell of fertilizer and the several mentions of a house that was white.

"Do you think they meant the White House, Mr Shipley?" she asked. A small crowd of dispatchers had gathered around her, sensing that this call was different.

"Call me Ben," said Saul charmingly. "And yes, obviously they meant the White House. That's why I'm calling you!"

Then Saul saw him, the same dark-skinned man who had come after him with a knife the night before. He was circling the painted bus, a gun in his hand.

"There he is, Penny girl!" Saul said softly but his words were drowned out by a sudden, loud sharp sound.

KAPOW!

The man had fired a bullet right through the front right tire of the bus. Was it perhaps too bald for the trip and needed changing? Or was he scrapping the mission? The sound was loud enough for the 911 dispatcher to hear it over the phone line. Her voice rose a notch.

"Goodness, what was that sound? Are you alright, sir?"

She twirled her finger high in the air, the signal to trace the call.

"I think one of them was firing at me. He might have seen me making the call." Saul cupped the mouthpiece and spoke to his dog. "That ought to light a fire under her."

"Please stay on the line, Mr Shipley," the dispatcher's voice came back. "Do not hang up!"

A moment later, she was back. There was a difference in her voice, something like urgency, even panic. "Hang on, sir. We're putting you through to the White House."

The tension in the Situation Room was palpable. Vice President Sam Steele and Karissa sat next to the phone. Five senior security officers stood close by. Steele had his tie pulled loose and even the normally impeccably turned out Karissa looked drawn. The past few nights she had made do with a mere three to four hours of sleep.

"Hang on, Mr. Shipley," Steele said, "I'm putting you on speakerphone. You're now speaking to us in the White House Situation Room. I'm Sam Steele —"

"Wait — you're really Vice President Steele?" said Saul, utterly incredulous.

"Yes, sir, and we appreciate your vigilance in making this call. I understand you believe the White House may be the target of some kind of attack?"

"Yes, sir, I'm convinced of it," said Saul. "I'm looking at a bus that's being loaded with some very odd hardware."

"When do you think this attack may happen?" Karissa asked. "Today? Tomorrow?"

"It's probably too late for an attack today," Saul reasoned. "The traffic will work against quick movement. I'd guess they wouldn't want to wait beyond tomorrow, though."

Of course, thought Karissa. *A Christmas day surprise.*

"Good thinking, Ben," said Steele. "You say the men look Middle Eastern? One of them tried to kill you a day ago?"

"That is correct, sir," said Saul.

"Tell me, does your area have buildings with rooftops?"

"Plenty of them, sir," said Saul eagerly. "This place is full of old brownstones and they all have roofs."

Steele put the phone briefly on mute as he looked up at the SWAT team Commander and got a nod back from him. "I think it's an immediate go for your sniper team, colonel," said Steele. "Godspeed and good hunting."

Into the phone, he said, "I want you to stay right where you are, Ben, and well away from windows. Don't get alarmed if you hear gunshots or sounds of explosions, just stay put. And once again, thank you for your service. Your country will remember you."

Petty Officer Christian Gabriel reached for his Navy-issue phone as he stepped out of the shower. That particular ringtone could only mean one thing. He glanced at the screen to confirm who was calling. The Office of the Vice President.

Christian had been up all night; no Christmas Eve festivities for him this year. He had spent the previous twelve hours in a Grumman C–2 Greyhound transport aircraft with five other men, representing the elite of Navy SEAL Team 6. They had returned just two hours ago to their Virginia Beach headquarters after another perfectly executed operation.

Steele spoke crisply. His instructions were clear.

"Yes, sir," said Christian, straightening to attention by habit. "Right away, sir. I understand, sir."

Maggie Gabriel was used to her husband coming home

at all hours of day and night. Twelve years of marriage had taught her that his job had no reliable appointment schedule or working hours. No weekend or holiday was sacred, not even Christmas Day.

She watched with some relief as he quickly dressed in his Navy service uniform. The khaki permanent-press shirt with dark trousers and black leather Eisenhower-style jacket suggested that his assignment was possibly less fraught with danger than usual. Maggie generally felt less worried when Christian set out in a more formal uniform. Navy combat fatigues were much more ominous.

Christian keyed the two deadbolts and entered the third bedroom of their Annandale, Virginia rancher located a half-hour away from the White House by government escort. He scanned the room and then went to work. Meticulously arranged around him was an arsenal of firearms and combat paraphernalia.

He quickly made several selections and left the room, double-locking the door behind him.

Pineapple Down

The Special Forces sniper adjusted his ear protection, checked the walkie-talkie clipped to his left shoulder and sat down on the small bench facing the brownstone's attic window. He nestled the aluminum alloy stock of his McMillan Tac-50 into his right shoulder and positioned the 24-inch barrel plus silencer extension on the sill. Through the eyepiece, he had a clear view of the boathouse's door, ajar and allowing an unobstructed view of his target, who was still seated inside the cab of the bus. The sniper waited patiently, finger resting lightly on the trigger, waiting for the signal from his brain.

After several minutes, the bus's door opened and the tattooed man with the horseshoe mustache stepped out, pushing the boathouse door wide open. He was now fully exposed.

This was the moment. The finger squeezed the trigger.

There was a muffled supersonic crack, almost entirely unnoticed in the early morning calm.

The bullet left the muzzle at 2,700 feet per second, forming a burst of smoke as hot gas met the cooler air. Upon impact the .300 Winchester hollow point mush-roomed inside the man's upper leg, exploding the flesh of his groin and shattering his femur as fragments of bone shredded his thigh. Blood gushed in a fountain from the severed femoral artery. The young man roared as he col-lapsed to the ground, sliding into a pool of his own blood.

The sniper leaned into his walkie-talkie. "Pineapple down. Repeat, Pineapple down."

Upon the pre-arranged signal, the strike team po-sitioned on rooftops and windows around the lot began moving quietly, quickly, towards street level, closing in on the boathouse.

At the same time, an older man wearing sunglasses ran towards the fallen body. No palpable pulse. Four younger men had run to the scene and stood some five feet away, stunned witnesses of the catastrophe.

The older man rose and pointed to the open door of the boathouse. The five men dashed inside, closing the door behind them. Rushing to the far corner of the building, they began to sweep the dirt away from a certain patch of earth until the handle of a trapdoor became visible. The old man wrenched it open, revealing a ladder going down a level. He signaled the others to go down first. Removing his sunglasses, he followed them, lowering the trapdoor behind him. The tunnel ran diagonally approximately 200 yards, ending in a one-car garage facing away from the street alongside another one of the condemned brownstones.

It was time to activate Plan B.

The old man had already bathed, shaved and dressed to take over should Plan A go south for any reason. And now his time had come. Breathing hard, he hoisted himself out of the tunnel and looked around. The dark, complex universe of his mind had now hard-boiled down to a single thought. The moment of *istishhad*, and his imminent martyrdom, was just hours away. He felt a cool, directed sense of purpose as if this was exactly the way it was supposed to be. His movements were precise and deliberate, his electric eyes darting efficiently around the dimly-lit garage. All appeared in order. The olive drab 2.5-ton utility cargo van stood there, freshly painted with the words 'Mobile Bomb Detection Unit' in large letters along the side. He climbed in behind the wheel and signaled to one of the men to raise the garage door.

The Hercules diesel sprang to life and the van moved out of its enclosure. Two hard left turns and then a right, and the vehicle was heading south just below the speed limit.

Washington, D.C.

1997

Merry Christmas

Through the tinted driver-side window, it was difficult to see the driver of the olive drab vehicle as it motored south on the Baltimore-Washington Parkway. Hunched forward, the older man looked keenly ahead as the cold, potholed asphalt slid rapidly beneath him at 60 mph. His ski cap was pulled over his ears and down over most of his forehead. His heavy, hooded sweatshirt covered his hirsute arms and read 'America the Beautiful' across the front. He was either growing a beard or in need of a shave, but either way, his numerous acne scars were less obvious.

It was serious business carrying a mixture of enriched uranium, ammonium nitrate derived from eighty bags of nitrogen fertilizer and two drums of fuel oil. All he needed to do was pull firmly on the hood latch just under the dash to fire the blasting cap and ignite a homemade 'dirty' nuclear bomb. The vehicle and driver would be instantly vaporized in an explosion reminiscent of the Oklahoma City facelift.

An hour passed. The man looked at his watch — plenty of time. He signaled to exit left off the parkway and in five minutes brought the official-looking vehicle to a stop behind a cluster of pine trees just inside the opened gate of Washington D.C.'s Fort Dupont Park. Well-concealed, he removed his ski cap and pulled off his hoodie, replacing them with a tan, official-looking shirt with a standup collar, a clip-on black tie and a crown visor cap that had been placed under the driver's seat. Now dressed for the work ahead, he was back on the parkway in minutes, four miles north of the intersection onto Pennsylvania Avenue.

Time: 10:40 am. Usual traffic.
Blood pressure 118/70.
Pulse 60 and regular.

As the vehicle turned onto H Street, the driver glanced right, noting the golden cupola of St. John's Episcopal Church with its bright yellow stucco walls. A blazing reminder of who the enemy was.

To hell with American Christians.

To his left lay Lafayette Park, with the towering bronze statue of President Andrew Jackson astride his stallion.

Death to American heroes.

He took a sharp left onto Jackson Place and headed south, past the massive tangle of columns and balconies of the Eisenhower Office Building. Up ahead was the white brick façade and green shutters of Blair House.

Loaded with sycophantic diplomats.

His lips tightened as he passed the 30-foot Colorado Blue Spruce, sparkling with 75,000 red and gold Christmas bulbs requiring no less than 80,000 watts of electrical power.

Santa Claus is coming to town.

He felt grateful, awash with a strange sense of peace. At the very last moment, he had been chosen for one of Allah's highest honors.

Ahead, he could see clearly the northwest gate to the White House and its sprawling West Wing.

Merry Christmas, Mr. President.

Time 11:18 a.m.

Right on schedule.

Split Second

It was unusual to have several busy workmen tending to the grounds behind the White House on Christmas morning. One was on a lawn tractor pulling a small wagon filled with tree trimmings, two were pruning bushes with what, from a distance, looked like electric hedge clippers, and two others were busy washing a row of lower windows with long-handled squeegees. Within view, leaning into the microphone clipped to his lapel, the White House rear sentry spoke crisply.

"Right on time."

The olive drab vehicle came to a stop out in the open at the first gatehouse. There was a presidential seal on the left lower corner of the windshield. The guard first inspected the windshield insignia and then squinted through the tinted window at the driver, who slowly wound down the window just enough to expose his upper chest and neck. His right hand now grasped and then swiveled the laminated photo identification card hanging from a chain around his neck so Christian Gabriel could see it.

Several things happened next, all in concert. The diesel engine roared as the vehicle lurched forward. Before it had advanced just two feet, its front tires were pierced by a row of saber tooth spikes, exploding both of them and instantly halting the vehicle. Then, in one coordinated, lightning-swift movement, the weapon was out of Gabriel's holster.

POW.

The compressed gas cartridge in the stun gun exploded and the two dart-like electrode projectiles struck the driver, one in the neck and the other on the left side of his chest. Immediately losing all voluntary control of his muscles, he slumped forward, rolling to the right and onto the floor.

Within seconds, the man riding the lawn tractor had grabbed the firefighter's super-ax from the cart and slammed it into the vehicle's front door, clawing it open. One after the other, the two window-washers next launched themselves through the opening and pulled the limp body of the driver out onto the lawn.

The third man was next inside the bus right behind a German shepherd dog that had emerged from the guardhouse and was standing over the now severed wire which ran from the emergency brake to the blaster cap next to a primer canister of C4 explosive.

The high-stakes split-second operation was over. Gabriel exhaled a sigh of relief: no friendly lives lost, always the most important component of a successful mission.

Vice President Steele and Karissa Smithson had elected to watch the operation from an upstairs window of the Executive Mansion. Steele had made a calculated assumption. "Taking the chance we could trap him out in the open would be risky but the mindset of a Jihadist suicide bomber has always been the same. Anything short of a perfectly executed mission is considered a failure."

The bomb squad had deactivated the dirty bomb. The discovery of the uranium sent chills down the spines of the two observers, who appreciated how close they had been to a nuclear explosion.

"The blast would have destroyed the south wall, taking the president and all of us with it," Steele said to Karissa, .

They entered the Situation Room, where the strike force had gathered.

"Good work, boys," said the Vice President, going around shaking each one's hand. "Our last-minute intelligence was solid and your actions were spectacular. You took the risk that we could trap him in the open and you pulled it off."

"I trust our target is not seriously injured?"

"We have him in high-security lock-up at the Central Detention Facility. The doctors are checking him now and then a suicide watch overnight," Gabriel replied.

"We'll interrogate him in the morning."

The Interrogation

The prisoner spent Christmas night in solitary confinement in an orange jumpsuit, his hands and feet shackled, his every move monitored via video feed by security officials in the surveillance room next door. Before dawn the next day, he was moved under armed guard to the interrogation room deep within the bowels of the Pentagon, where three well-muscled guards ushered him into a 14' x 14' room with a one-way mirror taking up an entire wall. A table and two opposing chairs were the only furnishings.

He was seated with his head bent downward, his chained wrists resting on the table. Bandages were visible on the left side of his neck.

"We've got you covered for every possible contingency," Steele said to Karissa. "But you can still change your mind.

Are you sure you want to go through with this?"

"I am the most qualified," Karissa replied, "I speak his language. If this man has information, I'm the only one who can get it out of him."

With that, Karissa entered the room.

She started with a perfunctory Arabic greeting as she moved toward the chair across the table from the man in orange. He made no attempt to speak, sitting with his head bowed.

"Where are you from?" Karissa started without preamble, speaking in Arabic.

No answer.

"You're not in a good position, I think you know that," she said. "However, if you cooperate, things might go just a little easier for you."

No answer.

"Do you have a name?"

No answer.

She leaned forward slightly and lowered her voice. She realized she would have to taunt a reply out of him.

"Allah gave you such a simple mission to carry out — and you couldn't do even that," she said. "Why didn't you pick someone more competent?"

The man raised his gaze for the first time to look into the eyes of his female interrogator. His eyes widened as a look beyond astonishment passed over his face, and he straightened, jerking his chained hand up to point at Karissa.

"You!" he bellowed. "It is you! You traitorous whore!"

Karissa gasped, every bit as taken aback as the prisoner, words suddenly failing her. How could she not have recognized her own father?

His face reflecting blinding rage, the old man let forth a roar from the depths of his being and lunged at his daughter, managing to reach across the table and throwing both manacled hands over Karissa's head to pull her towards him.

The two sharpshooters on watch just feet away outside the room did not lose a moment, squeezing off several rounds from their .357 Magnum Smith and Wesson pistols through vertical slots located in two corners of the room. An instant pink mist composed of vaporized blood, brain and bone filled the air. The jihadist's body caved forward before sliding down and hitting the floor first with what little remained of his face.

Karissa, caught in the arms of what now looked like a faceless dance partner gone limp, crashed atop her father.

The door to the small interrogation room burst open. Vice President Steele was the first to enter.

Body Shopping

He was not the kind who committed suicide. Besides, what purpose would it serve? True, the last 24 hours had been an unmitigated disaster, an unholy end to years of planning, training and money. He could not deny that. Still, he did not feel the holy heat of anger raging within his wretched French soul. He felt, instead, a cool and calculating mind, methodically examining options and immediate next steps. He was sure Allah the redeemer would give him a new opportunity to make good.

But then there was the thing in his shoulder, the chip planted there by that accursed Karima for whom he had done so much. He had not suspected its existence until a stray scratch had exposed it, leading to a festering sore. Though it burned like a scorpion's sting, he knew he would have to be clever about how he got rid of it. Thanks to that infernal GPS chip, his every move was being tracked.

Henri knew that he had to be careful about his movements. There was body shopping to be done. And there was no time to waste.

In a well-camouflaged room in Washington D.C., a bleary-eyed team of men, including Karissa and Vice President Steele, watched the moving green dot on the screen. Most of those present had not slept in over three days. The signal had traveled from the Druid Hill brownstones complex and was now tracking south to Baltimore's dangerous south-side inner city.

"He's still out there," Karissa said. Steele nodded, his hand rising to rub his shaved head out of habit. "Where on earth is he going?"

The pickup point under the Jones Falls Expressway in the worst part of Baltimore was the largest concentration of homeless persons in the city. Somehow they had to last out the winter. Each had a strategy; for some, it was a little help from a pint of white lightning or a bag of smack.

The Frenchman drove slowly through the community in his white van, scanning the homeless huddled in the dim recesses under the overpass. Some were too old, some too small, yet others too young. His eyes fell upon one who looked like he might do. He was just the right height, his physique matched and he seemed to have no obvious infirmities. On closer examination, he even seemed to have most of his teeth. His residence was a large cardboard box covered with a mud-splattered blue tarp. It stood in a shadowy corner away from the other homeless unfortunates who were huddled together around a flickering fire emanating from a rusty metal trash can. A pair of weathered green canvas army surplus tents closer to the fire represented the high rent district.

Parfait! The Frenchman could do his work unobserved and uninterrupted.

The hapless hobo's habit required two shots of the white stuff every day. Getting high was no longer the purpose; that quantity was just enough to fend off the wrenching stomach cramps, profuse sweating and diarrhea that came with withdrawal.

"Come on, *mon ami*, let's give your body what it needs," said the mysterious benefactor, his voice gentle and kind and just slightly accented as he administered the dose.

Twenty minutes later the homeless man, now hardly breathing, was in a lethal drug-induced coma, slumped on the floor of the van next to the driver's seat. Rigor mortis would not set in until three to four hours after he died. By then, with a little luck, some charred bones and teeth and the twisted metal of the van might be all that was left.

From an envelope, the Frenchman withdrew the GPS tracker chip, now tinged with his own dried blood, that he had extracted from between his shoulder blades earlier.

"Just so Ms. Smithson knows who you are," he muttered to himself.

A fleeting pleasurable memory flashed through his head of the last time he had made love to that heavenly young woman but was quickly replaced by a grim reminder of the treachery now in her heart.

"*Bise!*" he swore, as he placed the small electronic device in the tee shirt pocket of the now deceased homeless man.

He next turned his attention to the explosives, quickly attaching a magnetized brick-sized unit of high-grade composition C-4 to the underside of the front right fender. When it was remotely detonated by a signal from his cellphone a short while later the blast would not only incinerate the van and its contents but also take most of the north side of the Mulakat Café with it. *Quel dommage.*

The preparations complete, the man let himself into the driver's seat and pulled away. There was just one little thing left to do.

The van drove up to the Mulakat Cafe and reversed slowly into the alley next to the café's north side rear entrance. A passer-by might easily assume it was a supplier making deliveries. Indeed, the last step in the carefully orchestrated plan required the Frenchman to make sure that he was seen. He knew that someone would emerge from the restaurant's back door if he waited long enough.

Four minutes later, a man in his twenties, clearly of Middle Eastern descent, came out, pulling a cigarette from his pocket. The Frenchman was waiting, smoking a cigarette himself. He smiled a greeting and extended a lighter.

"Do you speak English?" he asked the young man, deploying an exaggerated French accent.

The young man shrugged. "What do you want?"

"Can I ask you a favor, my friend? Could you tell Mr Barhani that his mushrooms and lamb are here?"

"Why don't you tell him yourself?" asked the fellow.

The Frenchman looked at his watch. "I am running a little late," he said. "It would save time. I can start unloading by the time he sends his people to take an inventory and sign for the delivery."

"Ok, ok," said the boy peevishly. "But I need to buy a packet of cigarettes first from the corner store." Taking quick steps, he headed up the alley to the road and disappeared.

Eight minutes later the sound of an explosion shattered the peace of the neighborhood. A massive plume of black smoke rose from the northern end of the Mulakat Café.

In the White House surveillance room, the signal on the monitor suddenly disappeared. Steele arched an eyebrow in Karissa's direction.

"Did you see that?" he said softly. "Your Henri disappeared. Just like that."

The bomb squad and the forensic team reached the site of the devastation 14 minutes later. Only charred cinder blocks, molten metal, shards and shattered debris remained. The body inside the remains of the van was incinerated, leaving only some pulverized bones and a few teeth. There was no sign of a GPS chip.

The only indication of the dead man's identity came from a café employee who had stepped out of the café for some cigarettes and thus become the sole survivor of the blast.

"Yeah, there was a man in the alley," he told the investigating officer. "He had dark hair, medium build. He wanted me to give the boss a message about some delivery."

"Do you remember anything else about him?"

"Don't think so," he said, pondering for a moment. "No, wait. He spoke funny English. He had a funny accent. Like, I don't know, maybe French."

Cerebral Mush

"**Lance is going fast.**" Augusta turned to Cleo, her eyes misting. "He no longer recognizes me."

Cleo reached out and took Augusta's hand in hers. Her emotions were ambivalent — empathy for Augusta melded with bitterness towards her brother who had abused her, a sibling she had never loved.

"How much longer, Cleo?" Augusta asked.

As she squeezed Augusta's hand, Cleo searched for a shred of sympathy, forgiveness for the man lying on the bed, but found nothing in her heart.

The weeks following the Christmas attack had not been kind to Lance. Some inner switch seemed to have flipped, starting a deep slide into a cognitive wasteland. Cleo had seen variations of mental deterioration through her career but the swiftness of Lance's decline surprised even her.

She knew that the rot spreading through Lance's brain tissue would now be approaching a cerebral mush. His thoughts would be incoherent, streaming nonsense. Lance's arms, tremulous and wrinkled, now reached out to touch something, perhaps hallucinated butterflies. Gibberish emanated from his mouth.

A knock on the door of the presidential hospital suite snapped her back to reality. Sam Steele entered the room.

"See what's happened to him, Sam," Augusta said.

Steele looked down at the world's most powerful man and what he had turned into — the sallow color, the sunken cheeks, the distant stare.

Sam turned to Augusta and took both her hands in his. "I am so sorry, my dear."

With Administration approval, two professional colleagues recommended by Dr. Cleo Allworthy were appointed to assess President Lance Allworthy's state of mind and body. One was a neurology professor emeritus from Johns Hopkins University, the other a practicing psychiatrist and expert witness from Stanford renowned for his expertise in evaluating mental competence. No one was surprised when both doctors independently arrived at the same conclusion: Lance had irreversibly and completely lost it.

Their report read, in part —

... The President of the United States is suffering from a rapidly progressive form of incurable dementia and is no longer capable of making the judgments and decisions required for the performance of his duties as President of the United States. . .

"How much longer, doctor?" Augusta asked.

"Without intravenous hydration, we are usually talking less than ten days," said the physician. "The hospice protocol will make him more comfortable and certainly reduce the obvious agitation."

The news of Lance's mental and physical condition was announced within days to a shocked public that had been kept in the dark for much too long. With the President unable to discharge the powers and duties of his office, the Vice President would take over as President, in accordance with the 25th Amendment to the Constitution.

The bright noonday sun bathed the west front of the US Capitol, where a large gathering of the American political hierarchy stood solemnly. With his left hand on the Bible and his right hand raised, Sam Steele took the presidential oath of office as it was administered by the Chief Justice of the Supreme Court.

Do you solemnly swear to preserve, protect and defend the Constitution of the United States?

Samuel Steele spoke with clarity and conviction.

I do. So help me God.

Nothing to Hide

Cleo and Augusta rode back to the White House in silence.

It had not been an easy decision for Augusta to place Lance in hospice care for his remaining days. Sensing her anguish, Cleo reached for her hand, squeezing gently.

"You did right," she said. "He was so miserable."

"Strange, I don't feel sadness, " Augusta said. "I have some regrets of course, but I mostly feel relieved."

"Relieved?" Cleo probed gently.

"Our life together was a lie from the start. We had nothing important in common, hardly the perfect couple the public perceived us to be. No real partnership, no real love."

Cleo nodded letting Augusta continue.

"Over time, it even began to suit me strangely. Lance

avoided sex as much as he could — he was so insecure about his manhood and never really got over his perceived performance issues."

Augusta permitted herself a wan smile. "You know what's strange? I — I never once tried to reassure him. His insecurity was fine with me." She turned to look at Cleo. "Ahh — you probably think I'm an insensitive bitch."

Cleo ignored the remark and asked, "But why did you let him stew in his insecurity? Did you dislike him that much?"

"I don't think I ever hated Lance," said Augusta. "Even now. He just meant nothing to me."

"And — and I've always known," said Augusta, after a moment's silence, her voice a notch lower. "I've always known I was different."

"In what way?" asked Cleo, her heart suddenly racing.

"There was a day — I think it was the day I had my first kiss with some eager boy in high school — I knew that day that men did nothing for me. I felt real, complex, alive only when I was with a —" She didn't complete the sentence.

Cleo reached over and took Augusta's hand in hers. Neither spoke again until they reached the White House, nor did they need to.

Before she stepped out of the car, Augusta said, "I think I was drawn to the image and spectacle, the pomp and ceremony, being First Lady beside blond, blue-eyed Mr Perfect."

"And now all that's over," Cleo whispered.

Augusta nodded, "I feel as though a really heavy weight has just lifted from my shoulders."

With all the attention Lance's condition demanded, it had not occurred to Augusta that she would soon need to move out of the White House.

Lance's presidential suite was a mess.

"In the past month he refused to let anyone enter, not even the housemaid," said Augusta, surveying the chaos as they entered the room.

There was a faint and unpleasant organic smell in the air; unread newspapers were stacked high on the sofa in the sitting area; a soiled bathrobe lay at the foot of the bed, and there was half a glass of flat ginger ale by the bedside. The curtains were drawn and the room was dark but for an antique cloisonne lamp still lit on his desk, which was cluttered with notebooks, papers and pens.

Cleo sensed Augusta's paralysis. "I'll help you get this stuff organized."

Augusta just stood there shaking her head at the task in front of them.

"Come on now, Lewis and Clark started their expedition with a single step."

And so the clean-up began. They worked together for an hour, clearing the accumulated debris off the floor, straightening out the bed, putting away cutlery and dumping half-eaten food. While Augusta attended to the walk-in wardrobe, Cleo turned her attention to the desk, starting by sliding out its drawer, where her eyes fell on a buff-colored folder. Within were Lance's personal papers — a birth certificate, a marriage certificate, an expired driver's license and an outdated passport.

"The President, legally identified," Cleo muttered.

As Augusta walked up to join her, a single sheet fluttered out of the folder to the floor

"What's this?" Augusta said, picking it up. She read out loud from the printed sheet. "32 percent Great Britain; 18 percent Wales, Ireland, Scotland; 44 percent Scandinavian; 6 percent other."

She turned to Cleo. "Do you have any idea what this is?"

"Oh. My. God," Cleo whispered, hands to her mouth. "You should not have seen that."

"It has Lance's name on top, so no, I think I should have seen this. Are you going to tell me what it is?"

"You know what it is," Cleo said. "It's Lance's DNA report."

Augusta stared at the page again, remembering Katherine's surprise Christmas gift for everyone. Her eyes were transfixed on one number.

"Cleo —" she said. "It says here that Lance's genes are almost half Scandinavian. How can that be?"

"He did look a little like a Viking," Cleo said half jokingly, not enjoying the line of Augusta's inquiry at all.

"Did you know about this? Talk to me, Cleo!"

Smiling outwardly, Cleo was awash with anxiety. A part of her wanted to have no secrets from Augusta but another voice cautioned her that sharing a little could mean sharing a lot. What difference would it make anyway. Why should Augusta even care now?

"Well?" Augusta said. "I'm waiting."

Then, without warning, the words came tumbling out as the dam Cleo had held back for so long finally broke. Augusta, horrified and incredulous, listened as Cleo told the story of Lance's origin: his birth from the illicit relationship between a Scandinavian ne'er-do-well politician and his mother, a blonde, blue-eyed Swedish adulteress. The unfortunate genes he had inherited through that union predisposed him to the peculiar Nordic form of dementia known as Scanza Cerebral Dystrophy.

In the stunned silence that followed, it was minutes before Augusta found words again. "You held this terrible secret all these years," she said. "You mean Lance never knew?"

"I could not bring myself to tell him."

"Was this why you had such contempt for him? You and only you knew that the President of the United States was born a bastard child."

"No," Cleo said with the greatest reluctance. "I never looked down on Lance."

"You're right," conceded Augusta. "Not once have you

ever denied him when he insisted on his allergy shots. You even saved his life at that hotel when we first met."

"It was neither love nor kindness, Augusta," said Cleo, her voice a whisper. "I was always afraid of Lance. Only he knew my terrible secret shame. He blackmailed me with it all my life."

"Secret?" Augusta raised her eyebrow.

Cleo took both Augusta's hands in hers. "Lance knew. Like you, I have always been a woman's woman. But unlike you, I was taught to be ashamed of it. I lived in a dark closet, feeling empty and alone, hiding who I really am."

A tear trickled down Cleo's cheek.

Augusta reached around and pulled Cleo to her, "Silly girl!" she said. "You're not alone — there's two of us now. And you know something?"

She pulled Cleo's face close to hers, lips but an inch apart. Just before they kissed, she whispered, "There's nothing to hide anymore."

Rest in Peace

Whenever a new President takes office in the United States, one of the first things he is pressed to do is plan his own funeral. Lance had outlined an elaborate public extravaganza filled with fanfare and the orchestrated trumpeting of his legacy, whatever that would be. Now that he'd passed on, however, Augusta elected to take down the funeral's grandiosity a notch or three. For her, the event needed just a couple of days, regardless of whether you were mourning his death or celebrating it.

"I'd say one day lying in state in the East Room and then a day for the burial would be ample time," she said to Cleo. "The sooner we move on past this the better."

Media reporting on the funeral was mixed but the abbreviated funeral format did not go unnoticed. The *Wash-*

ington Examiner wasted no time in endorsing the two-day farewell to a 'do-nothing' president. Other editors and news anchors were less brutal, damning Lance with faint praise. A handful even gave Lance a pass, massaging the truth into less vindictive rhetoric. But without doubt, the common thread was that a mostly invisible president elected because of his golden-boy appeal and glowing promises had mostly proved to be an embarrassing illusion.

"It will mean so much to Augusta!" Kat said, adjusting her wide-brimmed black hat in front of the mirror.

"Can't disagree with that," said ET. "Though let's not forget how symbolic today's event will be for our little man." Almost four years old now, Bertram Haynes had never met his real father even once. Today he would attend his funeral.

The motorcade passed through the security gates of the West Point Cemetery overlooking the majestic Hudson River. It passed the Gothic Old Cadet Chapel and then made a right turn at the caretaker's cottage. A string of mausoleums and grave site memorials flanked both sides of the narrow road leading to a freshly dug grave. Uniformed soldiers saluted as the platinum coffin draped with the American flag was withdrawn from the stretch Cadillac hearse.

Augusta had reluctantly agreed to some of the ceremonial choreography Lance had wished for, including a traditional dirge played by the Marine band and a sky-shattering flyover of 21 fighter aircraft.

Augusta covered her ears, steadying herself against Cleo standing next to her. Their expressions were somber, as such occasions demand, but their eyes revealed a profound absence of grief. Kat even remarked to ET that she had never seen Cleo looking so much at ease. "I can't even remember the last time I saw her with make-up on," she whispered.

Before the casket was lowered into its resting place, the flag was removed and folded into a tight triangle and presented to the former First Lady, who passed it to Cleo. With a small shovel Augusta gently shoveled some soil on the casket as the priest began speaking. "We are gathered here to acknowledge the life of former President of the United States, Lance Allworthy. . . May God rest his soul . . ."

Samuel Steele and Karissa Smithson stood quietly looking on, with the Secret Service flanking both sides of America's new President. The two had expressed their condolences to Augusta privately the day before in the East Room.

Kat and ET were the first to embrace Augusta. Words were unnecessary and though everyone looked suitably austere, no one appeared overcome with sadness. Bertie, stranger to this strangest of moments in human life, stepped forward on his own towards Augusta, almost as though guided by some primal instinct, and opened his arms to her, smiling. With a small gasp, Augusta stooped to pick him up, "Oh, my dear sweet child."

Her eyes closed for a moment as her mind flooded with a swirl of unexpected maternal emotions.

"What should I call you?" Bertie asked her.

"Ummm," said Kat, pretending to contemplate. "I think Auntie might be nice."

Still holding him in her arms, Augusta looked into the child's polar blue eyes and kissed his wide forehead. She would have preferred Mama.

"I would like that," she said softly. "Perhaps on some weekends you could even sleep over at my house."

Bertie's eyes brightened, "Could I really?"

Augusta quickly looked towards Kat, who nodded, beaming. "You most certainly could, Master Bertie!" She raised her hand and the child gave her a joyous high-five.

"Would you allow your parents to join the sleepover?" Kat asked the child teasingly.

"Yes!" squealed Bertie, high-five-ing his mother now.

For a moment, all conversation was drowned out as the funeral ceremony ended with the traditional gunfire salute over the Hudson.

ET and Kat made their way back to the car, Bertie walking between them.

"Ahem," ET cleared his throat. "I was waiting until after the funeral to tell you. Your father just might have to miss a few of those sleepovers, young man."

Kat's eyebrow rose. "What's going on, soldier boy?"

"I was waiting to tell you," said ET, definitely uncomfortable. "The Pentagon apparently wants to pull me out of retirement. Some aerial surveillance work. They want Jack and me to team up again."

"Where?" asked Kat, eyes widening.

"Ermm — Serbia was mentioned," said ET.

Kat's jaw dropped as she opened the passenger side door and got in, fastening her own seatbelt as she looked back at ET placing Bertie in his car seat.

"You will not be going to no Serbia any time soon, Mr. Haynes — and that's an order!" she said firmly, "And I have Bertie's full support on this."

ET slid into the driver's seat tossing off a salute. "Whatever you say, General!"

He nodded as he turned the key to start the car and smiled. "Perhaps President Steele will have to manage this country's foreign affairs without my help."

"Indeed he will," Kat said.

Augusta and Cleo had no interest in being at the funeral a moment more than strictly necessary but protocol demanded that they wait until everyone had left. A light late-morning rain had started up, making Cleo pop open an umbrella to shelter Augusta and herself. It seemed like an eternity but finally the mourners had all bid their adieus.

All except one. He stood beside Lance's grave, clutching

a bouquet of daffodils. His thinning mix of wavy blond and gray hair was damp from the rain and his disheveled appearance suggested he might have slept in his clothes.

As though sensing their attention, the man laid his flowers down on the grave and stood, staring at the two women. His brilliant glacier-blue eyes were a stunning contrast to his tired, weathered face and rumpled attire.

They stood like that for the longest moment staring at each other, the stranger, the widow and the dead man's sister. Then the old man nodded his head somewhat formally in their direction and with a curious dignity walked away.

"Was that —?" Augusta began.

"Yes," said Cleo, reaching for her hand. "I'm sure it was."

"But if he was Lance's father — I don't understand," said Augusta. "Why hasn't he succumbed to the same disease?"

"The genes that cause the disease express themselves variably from generation to generation," Cleo said, simplifying it for Augusta. "Sometimes the genes are passive. With Lance, they were not."

"Poor man," said Augusta. "He looks like an utter failure. A man who achieved nothing in his life."

"Yes," agreed Cleo. "Nothing except father a West Point superstar who became the President of the United States."

Busted

Breathless and hungry, Karissa and Sam Steele approached the end of their favorite Rock Creek Park trail, passing under Pennsylvania Avenue less than a mile from the White House. The Secret Service had finally persuaded the President to abandon the highly predictable and, in their minds, dangerous stop for pastry and coffee outside Nathaniel's Dog Tag Bakery. The pastries were now delivered to the White House.

This Sunday's jog had been free of the usual casual conversation. It was typically Steele who would start the banter but this particular morning he seemed different, withdrawn. But of course the most powerful man in the world has every right to be lost in his own thoughts, Karissa reasoned. It was a wonder how he managed to stay so even-keeled with all that he had going on in his head.

Her mind strayed to thoughts more personal. *What did she mean to this inscrutable man?* He had always been proper in every way, always respectful. If he had any real feelings for her, he had displayed none of the usual signs that point towards a romantic interest. Yet, somehow, time after time, it was always Karissa by his side at events, meetings, ceremonies and yes, every Sunday morning.

A small voice told her that this was destined to lead nowhere, whether or not the attraction she felt for him was reciprocated. Good thing she had not told him certain details about her life and her family other than that her father was no longer a part of it and that her mother lived alone somewhere abroad. She was thankful that he had not pressed her for more details.

They rode back from the park to the White House in silence. Once there, Karissa stepped aside into the powder room off the foyer to freshen up before making her way to one of the easy chairs in the living room.

The presidential quarters reminded her of a bachelor pad: colorless and artless, the furnishings stiff and the floor coverings plain. This was the habitat of a man who needed a woman's touch in his life. *Could she be that woman? Was she in love with Samuel Steele? Was it her love that had kept her from burdening him with the messy details of her past?*

What was that thumping in her chest?

Bakery aromas wafted out of the kitchen. Steele emerged from the kitchen and moved toward the lounge chair directly across from Karima. In contrast to her, he seemed at ease and in control, a man on top of his game.

"All set to hit the pastry now?" he asked.

"No, thank you."

Her heart was pumping wildly now. How could she possibly be this man's friend and withhold from him such important things about herself? He trusted her. She could feel his comfort with her, his affection for her. Whether he loved her back or not, he deserved better than lies, even lies of omission.

"Mr President," she began. "Sam —"

"Yes," he said, pastry plate still extended, eyebrow raised. "What is it?"

Karissa took a deep breath. "There is something —" she began. "That is to say, I have something to tell you."

"Well, I'm right here and waiting," he said.

"My real name is not Karissa Smithson," she blurted out.

The expression on Steele's face turned serious. "Now is that a fact, Ms. Smithson?" he said. "Would that mean you have been lying to the US government all this time while sitting in one of its highest security jobs?"

She nodded, trembling. She looked down at her feet. She had lived with the fear that someday the shoe would drop and her world as she currently knew it would come to an end. Now she was ready for whatever would come next.

"Hmmm," said Steele, steepling his fingers. "This is

most upsetting. And of course, unexpected. I would say I am extremely disappointed."

Karissa said nothing, looking down.

"Would it also be true then that your real name is, let me guess now, Karima Salmady?"

Startled, Karissa looked up.

"And is it or is it not true that you were brought up in Beirut?"

She said nothing, her mouth open.

"I thought as much."

How much more did he know? Karissa waited for what would come next, her chest wrenching tighter.

Can he hear my heart hammering?

She waited.

When he spoke next, his voice was grave.

"It's not easy to put one past US security operations, Karima," he said. "Apparently, our friend Henri had not factored that in when he orchestrated his plan to insert you into the upper ranks of our government. While your credentials appeared impeccable when you first arrived in this country right up to the time you received a high-level security clearance, a recent event raised red flags and questions about who you really are."

Karima listened, stone-faced. Finally, it was happening — the unraveling of her life in America.

"Your alleged husband, Lieutenant Smithson, had been designated by the Department of Defense as missing in action or a prisoner of war — until his remains were found in a cave along with some twenty others in the mountainous region of Rwanda north of Kigali where he went missing eight years ago.

"The estranged wife of Lieutenant Smithson has come forward with a child whose DNA matches that of the husband you had declared as yours. This woman, who is still his wife, has claimed his remains."

Karissa, back to Karima now, looked up at him. "What else do you know?"

"Karima," said Sam, almost rolling the syllables in his mouth to feel them. "It seems so strange to think of you as not being Karissa any more. And yes, I not only know what your real name is but I also know everything about you that really matters."

"About my relationship with Henri?"

"We know you had one and that it was close. We don't know the details."

Karima looked up, locking her eyes on his. Steele's expression seemed to soften.

As though he had pressed a button, Karima's floodgates opened then. In the next few minutes, all the secrets of her relationship with Henri came tumbling out in an unfettered explosion of words and feelings. How he had groomed her, their romance, how she had blossomed under his mentoring and how he had eventually used her and her family. The fake identity Henri had created for her, her mission to America; her early days, the before and after of the moment she had planted the GPS in Henri's shoulder.

And somewhere along all that, she found herself speaking of her growing love of America, and her deep need to be cleansed of the betrayals of her trust and love.

Nodding with each revelation, Steele allowed Karima to unburden herself of all the things he already knew before he spoke again.

"But Karima, I know something more than all that about you. I know that — you are an American patriot. You've worked tirelessly in the defense of America. When we learned about your past, I already knew that you were the victim here, not the perpetrator. I knew then and I know now that you are an invaluable asset." He seemed to hesitate.

"Is there something more?" she asked.

Suddenly, the most powerful man on the planet seemed to be searching for words. "Yes, there is." Sam Steele took a deep breath and looked straight into Karima's eyes. "I also know that I care for you very much."

Startled, she looked up. "Wh-whaat?"

"I know too that I have been in your dreams for a long time," he said, his voice stronger now. Karima shook her head from side to side and sighed.

"Oh Sam, what happens now? What I did was wrong. Ignorance and innocence are not a defense. Actions should have consequences, no matter who it is."

A long silence sat between them, the kind that happens between lovers who must face difficult realities.

"There will be an investigation and a congressional hearing," Steele said. "It will be a formal inquiry. The process will take its own course and at times you will find yourself standing in a harsh light."

Karima nodded. "I understand."

"But know this," Sam continued. "When the truth comes out, you will spread your wings again. I am in your camp and I want you to know that all will end well for you."

He allowed those words to sink in before he added, "Everything will end well for us."

The President stood and walked across the living room to the foyer and opened the door. Two uniformed men stepped inside.

"Sergeants Brady and Sullivan will take over from here."

It's For You

"Happy Birthday, sweetheart!" Sam said as Madalena, Karima's mother, entered the room with a large chocolate cake blazing with candles. Written across the cake in cursive vanilla-cream script were the words *Happy 43, Karima!* and below it, *10 September 2001*.

"Yes, happy birthday, my sweet Mima!"

Karima laughed, "Who needs birthdays anymore, except for the cake? MumMum, you make my sweet tooth dance with happiness."

"Even better than a Natty pastry," Sam said smiling.

"Our jog this morning allows for an extra large piece, you know," Karima announced.

"But of course." Sam said, licking his lips.

Karima leaned in to blow out the candles, her glowing

cheeks and dancing eyes highlighting her happiness.

Almost three years had passed since she had been pardoned for her connection to Henri Duchamp, the man now known as the mastermind behind the failed attempt on the White House and President Allworthy's life. With President Steele's hand quietly on the tiller the inquiry into her relationship with Duchamp had been managed without undue spectacle or scandal, and concluded with a presumption of innocence and a special acknowledgment of her role in thwarting the infamous Christmas attack. Oddly, the biggest bureaucratic hurdle had been the changing of her name back to Karima Salmady.

The remaining years of Sam Steele's presidency were deemed a clear success as he navigated the country out of the troubled waters his predecessor had left it in. However, much to the surprise of an adoring public he opted not to run for a second term in favor of a more private life free of the turbulence of American politics.

Karima had chosen to continue her work for the Department of Defense in the service of the much smaller Central Intelligence Agency as the most respected of Arabic interpreters. Despite the hard work, she had aged well. At 43, she brought a new level of elegance to the word 'beautiful', her glossy, thick black hair completely free of gray.

Karima's phone came to life as she swallowed the last mouthful of birthday cake. The irritating chirping sound meant that the call was coming via the high-security CIA chat server. Steele brought the phone over to her. "It's for you, birthday girl."

"Hmm," she said, entering the 12-digit passcode and pushing her reading glasses up the bridge of her nose.

Birthday greetings, ma cherie!

Who is this? she tapped into her phone.

Moments passed and then the words appeared: *What do you say we get together and celebrate? Just like old times?*

"What's wrong?" Karima's mother asked, aware that her daughter looked suddenly distressed.

Karima said, "Someone has hacked my phone."

The message continued.

What do you think of a cozy dinner in New York? I know the perfect spot. They have the best Flounder and Prawn Almondine, my sweet. Your favorite!

Karima exclaimed, "It's him, Sam. It's Henri. He's alive and wants to meet."

"What the —" said Steele, looking stunned.

A small ping signaled a new message.

I've taken the liberty of reserving a table for us at one of the world's finest restaurants.

Ping!

You must know it — Windows on the World. The view is spectacular.

Karima turned to Sam. "Windows on the World?"

"Classy place, with a God's-eye-view of New York. I think it takes up the entire top floor of the building."

"What building?" Karima asked.

"One of New York's finest landmarks." Sam said.

"The North Tower of the World Trade Center."

Epilogue

2022

Prelude to terror

This novel is a work of fiction and not based on any actual incident. None of the characters are intended to resemble any person living or dead. The main event described — a dry run leading up to the 9/11 attack on the World Trade Center — is entirely a product of my imagination.

However, there is nothing imaginary about the terrorism that has now become a sad fact of everyday life in the

United States and across the globe. Suicide bombers wearing lethal vests, holy warriors armed with car bombs and modern guns, rampant subversion, double-dealing and lethal conflicts are sadly part of our current reality.

There once was a time, not so many years ago, when suicide bombers were unheard of and the American way of life was not every terrorist's favorite target. Indeed, to many of us, history is divided neatly into two eras — before 9/11 and after. The age of terrorism began with the crashing of an American Airlines Boeing 767 into the North Tower of New York's World Trade Centre right before the world's eyes.

Indeed, 9/11 was the most audacious and organized terrorist attack in American history but it was certainly not the first. The roots of terrorism and anti-Americanism depicted in my story go back to the iconoclastic 1970's.

It was a period that changed the geopolitical trajectory of the United States forever.

The beginnings were almost innocuous; no one could have predicted that the separate threads that evolved in the United States, the oil producing countries of OPEC, the Middle East and Southeast Asia would lead to the terrorized world as we know it today.

The 70's were a time of exuberance, experimentation and activism in America. On the one hand, Star Wars, pop art and a photograph of a naked John Lennon on the cover of Life magazine defined a generation pulsing to new rhythms from Stevie Wonder funk to Rolling Stones rock. A generation that often viewed a utopian world through the filter of mind-altering drugs like LSD. A generation that contained some 40,000 diverse tie-dyed, Birkenstocked Americans who spent a rainy, historic weekend at Woodstock, New York, immersed in the spirit of love, peace and music.

On the other hand was an America convulsed with domestic unrest fired by opposition to the endless war in Vietnam, gay and women's rights, Roe v. Wade, massive inflation and the implementation of the Civil Rights Act.

As the first stirrings of anti-American sentiment began to be felt in the Middle East, one could say the epicenter of those feelings might have been in Lebanon, where, as my story depicts, a devastating, multi-sectarian civil war erupted in 1975, mainly between an influential ruling elite of Maronite Christians and the country's large but marginalized Muslim population. An influx of Palestinian refugees had swelled the ranks of the Muslims, bringing Israel into the fray, with America soon following suit.

What started as Lebanese civil unrest quickly acquired international stakeholders.

The beautiful and historic capital city of Beirut sustained major damage with relentless shelling and the killing of over 66,000 men, women and children during the bloody course of the conflict. The downtown area became a dangerous no-man's land separating Muslims in the west of the city and Christians in the east.

By June 1982, 100,000 Israeli troops and over 500 fighter aircraft occupied West Beirut and with the help of US and French peacekeeping forces there, they forced the withdrawal of the defeated Muslims from Beirut.

The first recorded terrorist attack against America occurred in April 1983, when Muslim militants detonated car bombs near the French and American barracks in east Beirut. The devastating second attack in Beirut witnessed in our story by ET Haynes and Jack Goodwell came six months later, in October of that year.

A nascent Islamic militant group known as Hezbollah took responsibility for this attempt to force the United States out of Lebanon.

This was the first ever suicide bombing attack against America. Though no one realized it, the world had just entered a dangerous new age of terror and anti-Americanism.

The 1990s was the decade in which sporadic terrorism morphed into the fanatic, US-hating global movement we know it to be today. The United States had come into focus as the singular target of terrorists worldwide. Any US institution or US citizen was fair game.

How did this happen?

The roots go back to 1979, when the Soviet Union invaded Afghanistan, bringing the prospect of yet another communist nation onto the world stage. As it had in Vietnam (and in Korea), the US could not stand by idly and watch their arch-enemies over-run another nation, despite domestic sentiment in the US being against another war.

A counter-resistance had already formed in Afghanistan: the *mujahideen* or 'freedom fighters' were a growing army of Muslim fighters who saw a Soviet-controlled Afghanistan as the death of everything they valued. And here the US — the CIA in particular — saw an opportunity for a proxy war.

With generous funding from the United States funneling through Pakistan — which was happy to pocket large sums en route — as well as weapons and training, the *mujahideen* became a formidable Muslim force, eventually beating back the Soviets after a protracted conflict.

Significant US funds had been directed to several select "freedom fighters" highly regarded by the CIA at that time. Unknown to the US, they were using American money to support and build up a jihadist group called Al Qaeda, led by a moody, wealthy, 6'5" Saudi engineer named Osama bin Laden who was much agitated by what he saw as the growing threat of US dominance in the Muslim world.

In 1996, bin Laden emerged on the world stage when he issued a *fatwa* — a decree — calling for a global jihad or holy war against the "treacherous, brutal and greedy" United States for occupying Muslim holy lands within Saudi Arabia.

"We will destroy, fight and kill the enemy until by the

grace of Allah it is completely defeated," he swore.

Authorized by President Obama, on May 2, 2011, the Navy's SEAL Team Six, piloting two Black Hawk helicopters, descended on bin Laden's secret compound in Abbottabad, Pakistan, and gunned down the 54-year-old godfather of modern radical Islamic terrorism. His second-in-command, Egyptian terrorist and bin Laden's private physician, Ayman al-Zawahri immediately took over the Al Qaeda terror network, eventually seeking refuge in Afghanistan after America's bungled withdrawal on August 30 2021. He was killed in July the following year by a Hellfire drone strike authorized by President Biden.

History has revealed that the real mastermind behind 9/11 was not Osama bin Laden but rather Khalil Sheikh Mohammed, a Pakistani graduate of a technical university in North Carolina, who conceived of the 'Plane Operation' and proposed it to Bin Laden in 1996. Captured after 9/11 in 2003, KSM, as he is now called by many, ironically has spent more than 20 years in the US Navy detention camp in Guantanamo Bay, Cuba, facing the death penalty with five other defendants. As of May 2022, a jury has not been selected for the trial, but will be scheduled in 'due course'. The delay, it has been reported, is the result of a carnival of legal miscarriages from military judges recusing themselves or resigning, to the question of what is admissible evidence and what is considered classified, to the ravages of Covid-19.

The well-respected Cato Institute argued in 2017 that after nearly 15 years and a staggering $5 trillion spent on its War on Terror, the USA is not significantly safer. Sadly, it seems the US policies of reshaping the Middle east through military interventions and nation building have both arguably worsened the situation. Strong-arming countries of the Middle East and interfering in their politics seems to have only exacerbated the very resentments that led to anti-American sentiment and terrorism in the first place. Not only has the US not succeeded in spreading democracy to any nation it tried to "rebuild" but it also left those countries worse off than it found them. Iraq, for example, now fields multiple internal terror threats from ISIS, the al Qaeda and other newly-formed terrorist groups. Terrorism has become a game anyone can play even without formal affiliation, as long as the target is vaguely seen to be American, western, oppressive or in some way imperial.

America's abandonment of Afghanistan into Taliban hands after decades of costly war, training and attempts to spread "democracy" is the best illustration of a failed 2 trillion dollar strategy. Together, Korea, Vietnam, Iraq and Afghanistan represent global wars that in my opinion, the US should not have fought and did not win, and which only served to fan the flames of anti-Americanism. At the time of this writing the extent and nature of America's involvement in Russia's invasion into Ukraine remains to be seen.

It is not my intention here to write a thesis on the origins and future of terrorism but I wanted the reader to understand why I set my story in Lebanon, where the seeds of anti-American terrorism were first sown. Since then, we have watched the end of cherished ways of life, the rise of outrage and anti-Americanism, as well as a new and more treacherous planet.

I created Lance Allworthy, my fatally flawed American president, to underscore the kind of leadership I believe we desperately need today — unselfish, knowledgeable, compassionate and competent. Ironically, these are the very qualities embodied by Samuel Steele, Lance's successor. We need a return to a functioning, responsive government if we are ever to become a safer, kinder nation again.

Henri Duchamp, the suave French villain of my story, was inevitable. He represented the best and the worst of the west — the inner conflicts, the pitting of religions against each other and, ironically, a collision between the west and the east, all within the same mind.

I created this small parallel universe based on an imagined dry-run leading up to the world's most tragic terror event on September 11, 2001.

The rest is history.

Gratitude

On a rainy afternoon in March 2017 after 50 years of practicing medicine it was time to pack it in. Jerry B. was my last patient, a vibrant man in his late seventies. We had developed over time a special relationship based on our mutual interest in photography. That afternoon Jerry informed me that he was busy writing a book, a mystery. His plan was to write a mystery every year for the next 12 years, putting him at age 90 or thereabouts when he finished the series.

I was struck by his contagious sparkle, energetic optimism and complete lack of regard for his date of birth.

Despite being close to his age, I was inspired by him to write a book of my own.

Sadly Jerry died the following year but not before he had read the first draft of my magnum opus, offering the charitable comment "An ambitious start". Somewhat like a difficult pregnancy with an array of pre-existing conditions ranging from no typing skills to an initial lack of understanding as to what actually goes into creating a story that might qualify as a novel, it has taken me five years to deliver *Fatally Flawed*. Five years of rewrites, fits and starts, detours, distractions, dead ends, rearrangements and reverses.

Besides Jerry's spark that got me airborne, I owe thanks to many other people who have offered their encouragement and assistance along the way. Among them: Roger Dudik, Nadene Seiters, Susan Dimond, Barbara Bernhardt, Curt Kane, Melissa and Ralph Panebianco, Ron and Elaine Kreiling, Alden and Judy Irons, Marilyn Arseneau, Deno Trakas, John Warley and Jonathan Haupt, Executive Director of the Pat Conroy Literary Center.

Being blessed with special circumstances also helped the writing process: the absence of a job, Covid-19 and an obsessive-compulsive personality. After all, if Shakespeare could knock out Romeo and Juliet during the bubonic plague perhaps I could crank out a story during a two-year pandemic.

And then comes C Y Gopinath, my editor, mentor and dear friend whose dedication, enthusiasm and countless recommendations made my story a much better one. I am also most grateful to him for his assistance with the final formatting and design of the book.

But most of all, my deeply felt thanks go to my wife Nancy, a critical reader, for her boundless patience, steadfast support and intuitive insights.

About the Author

Robert Lisle is a graduate of Williams College and Columbia University Medical School. He is also an Air Force Viet
Nam veteran. He retired after practicing family medicine
for over 50 years. He has had a lifelong passion for photography and its history, and has written and lectured exten-
sively on the subject.

Robert Lisle lives in the beautiful Lowcountry of South
Carolina with his wife Nancy.

Fatally Flawed is his debut novel. He is currently developing
his next thriller, with the working title of *Coming Home*.